ORC'S CRAVING

MONSTER MATE HUNT, BOOK 1

AVA ROSS

ENCHANTED STAR PRESS, LLC

For my own special hero,
my husband, Rusty.

SERIES BY AVA

Mail-Order Brides of Crakair

Brides of Driegon

Fated Mates of the Ferlaern Warriors

Fated Mates of the Xilan Warriors

Holiday with a Cu'zod Warrior

Galaxy Games

Alien Warrior Abandoned/

Shattered Galaxies

Beastly Alien Boss

Bride of the Fae

A Sci-Fi Holiday Tail

Monsterville, USA

Monster on Board

(co-written with Alana Khan)

A Monster Worth Fighting For

(Monster Between the Sheets)

Love at First Orc

Monster Mate Hunt

Single Titles
Dad Bod Dragon
Mated to the Dragon
Jasmine's Enchanted Genie
Swamp Thing (You Make My Heart Sing)

You can find her books on Amazon.

ORC'S CRAVING

On the night of the Monster Mate Hunt, I'll be claimed as an orc's bride.

Rhoslyn

When my sister is chosen for the Monster Mate Hunt—an annual event where two women must sacrifice themselves to the orcs for the good of us all—I volunteer in her place. The orcs hunt me as I bolt through the forest. I'm captured by the gruff, growly Commander Jaus, who expects me to cook and clean, plus sleep in his quarters with him at night, despite insisting he doesn't want a mate.

Then something changes, and his dark, brooding gaze turns my way . . .

Jaus

Rhoslyn's beautiful, spitting mad, and determined never to be my bride. I take her to my home in the orc city, and in no time, I long for what I don't deserve—a mate and a life full of joy. When the city's attacked, and her life is in danger, I'll destroy everything just to protect her. I'm going to defeat our enemy, and then I'm going to make Rhoslyn mine.

Orc's Craving is Book 1 in the Monster Mate Hunt Series. Expect fated mates, found families, a distinctive size difference, and a "touch her and die" hero. Each book is standalone, but the series is best if read in order.

Books in Order:
Orc's Mate
(a prequel novel – FREE with newsletter sign-up)

Orc's Craving
Orc's Fate
Orc's Maiden
Orc's Captive
Orc's Taming

CHAPTER I
RHOSLYN

A blood-ringed sun set on the evening of the Monster Hunt. Once darkness cloaked our world, two women from our village would leave the safety of the high fortress walls to become brides to vicious, powerful orcs.

No one knew for sure what happened after they stepped beyond the walls, because the women were never heard from again.

With my basket of herbs hooked over my arm, I hurried along the winding forest path that twisted like a serpent through the undergrowth. Sunlight pierced through the dense canopy above, casting eerie shadows that darted among the ancient trees. Silence loomed over the woods, broken only by my light footsteps, a random chirp of a bird, and the squawk of a squitt hiding among the upper branches overhead. Nature itself seemed to hold its breath.

It never paid to remain beyond the safety of the fortress walls when darkness swallowed the world, and not just because of the Hunt.

The shaydes stalked us, hunting for food. We were their prey.

My knife gripped tightly in my hand, I left the depths of the forest and rushed across the broad grassy area between the woods and the high fortress walls.

Mine was the only village in this area, though I'd heard there were other villages far away. Only a few from my village had traveled in that direction, however.

Over a thousand humans hid beyond the ring of stone, relying on the fierce, enormous orcs who granted us protection from creatures even more dangerous than them in exchange for brides.

I slipped through the well-guarded door.

"Rhoslyn," the guardsman said with a glare, stomping forward. "Why do you challenge them like this?"

"What do you mean?" I asked breezily, slipping my knife into the sheath strapped about my waist and brushing evergreen needles from my long blue skirt. I'd collected those while digging roots at the base of the tree. "I found some willadon." I lifted the chunk of gnarly black root from my basket. "Now I can make more tea for your mother."

His lined face softened. "You're too kind to us all."

"I love brewing potions and making tinctures that help my friends."

"And what about Rhoslyn? What do *you* want for yourself?" His pale blue eyes like my own softened, and his voice took on a fatherly tone.

I placed the root back in my basket with the herbs I was eager to dry. "I want to watch my sister marry the man she loves and spend the rest of my years bouncing her babies on my lap. And discover new uses for herbs."

"No marriage and bouncing babies for you?"

I winced. "I'm twenty-five. Who would have me?"

"Many. If you went to the village dances, you'd find a man to love."

"I don't need a man to make me feel complete."

"What about children? Surely you wish to raise young."

I did long for a child, but I'd yet to find anyone I dared give my heart to.

"Lyneth weds in a few months, does she not?" he asked.

Thinking of how happy my pretty sister would be with the man she loved, I grinned. "That's correct."

He patted my arm. "And then she'll move in with him and leave you alone. That would be the time to find your own husband."

My chin lifted. "I like being alone." Most of the time. Too often, I was lonely. "I plan to trade a tincture for a chall kit. The fluffy beast will make a nice companion."

"Indeed, the small creature will, but I haven't given up on you yet. Someone will offer for your hand." His warm gaze held appreciation, though it didn't feel slimy like—

Kael's eyes sharpened as he gazed past my shoulder.

Heavy footsteps approached, and my shoulders curled. If only I could sink beneath the cobblestones. I didn't need to turn; I knew who stalked closer.

I pivoted, my hand going to my knife, though I didn't pull it. That might get me into more trouble than I was eager to take on at the moment. But the last thing I wanted to do was present my back to Eamon, our village mayor.

"There you are, Rhoslyn." His greasy tone made my skin twitch.

Last night, this man cornered me in an alley and pressed his thick lips against mine. His hands roamed my body until I thrust my knee between his legs. With his barks of anger echoing around me, I rushed home, where I locked the door and leaned against it, trembling with rage and dismay.

Not long ago, he told me I'd soon be his bride.

He said he wouldn't ask permission, that he'd take me to his home, and no one would stand up for me.

He also told me if I didn't allow him to do as he pleased, he'd hurt my sister.

"I'm sorry, Eamon. I must return to my home right away." I held up the root, hoping he wouldn't see the quake in my hand. "Kael's mother needs her tea, or her body will ache all night." I forced a cheerful smile onto my face. "We wouldn't want to leave an elder in pain, now would we?"

Eamon huffed, and his gaze traveled down my curvy frame. "The women have been chosen."

Kael bristled, stomping his feet and clutching his weapon. "We should tell the orcs no. We've sacrificed our women to them for ten years. It needs to end!"

"If we don't fulfill our side of the truce, the orcs will withdraw their protection." Dread coiled tightly around my heart. "We'll be overrun and consumed by the shayde before we can suck in a deep breath."

But did the fates help the woman claimed during the hunt?

Kael's shoulders slumped. He knew we had no choice. "Who must go into the woods tonight?" The fear in his voice told me he prayed one of the chosen wasn't his only daughter.

No one wished to become the mate of an orc. Why would they?

Our elders spoke of them in hushed whispers, and parents used tales of them to make their young behave. Some said they lived in splendor in a shining kingdom near the sea, while others said they were enormous, hideous beasts who lived in stark, damp caves.

They said that those claimed during the hunt were rutted until they became pregnant with an orcling. Once they gave birth, they'd be rutted again. Over and over until the day they died.

"Calita is the first. Her mother clings to her, but her

father will see the deed done." Eamon's sly gaze met mine. "The name of the other woman who must leave the safety of the fortress and become the bride to an orc is being notified at this moment."

"Who is it?" Kael bellowed, his weapons clattering against his side.

The slick smile Eamon sent me made my pulse come to a jarring halt. My mouth went dry, and my throat clogged off with terror.

"No," I growled, knowing immediately who he meant. "Lyneth plans to wed soon."

"Lyneth will do as she's told." He chuckled, low and nasty. "The orcs won't care if she loves another when they capture her and claim her on the forest floor. I hear their bodies are large *everywhere*. That they don't take time to . . . shall we say, ensure a woman is eager to receive their favors."

Rage poured through me, making my face sting. Dropping my basket, I stomped over to him, sliding my knife from its sheath. If I gutted him this instant, I'd not only avoid lying beneath him on his bed one day soon, but I might also have a chance to save my sister. "I. Said. No!"

He backed up, his lips twisting. "It's not your decision, woman."

"It is if I volunteer for the hunt in her place."

Kael gasped. "No, Rhoslyn. You cannot."

"Anyone but Lyneth." I gripped my blade so hard it made my hand ache.

"You have no choice in this matter," Eamon said.

Oh, but there was always a choice. No one had ever volunteered, but there was nothing in the agreement that said a woman couldn't. I'd read the passage in the scrolls myself.

I sucked in a bitter breath and shoved it from my pinched lungs. "*I volunteer.*"

"Are you sure?" Eamon asked. "You may have a better offer to consider."

"I'd rather gut myself than marry *you*," I bit out.

"Very well, then." Eamon latched onto my arm and shoved me toward the gate, Kael followed, uselessly protesting. "The sun has nearly set. You must leave now."

My eyes stung with tears, and I struggled to break free of his grip. "But Lyneth. At least let me tell her goodbye."

"I'll tell her you took her place." Kael's warm gaze met mine. "I'll protect her too." He glared at Eamon. "She'll move in with me until she marries."

"Thank you." Breaking free of Eamon's biting nails, I hugged Kael, whispering a heartfelt plea. "Tell her I love her, would you? That I'll come back."

"I will." His face cratered with grief. He didn't need to name it. We all knew.

No women had ever returned from the hunt.

CHAPTER 2
JAUS

"You don't need to watch over me," Prince Madr said firmly from where he sat on a thick tree branch beside me.

I appreciated that he didn't look down his broad nose at me like the king. "You know I do. Your father gave the order himself."

"*Our* father," he said with a lift of his thick brow.

Only Madr acknowledged our shared blood. The rest of the kingdom might whisper about my parentage behind closed doors, but any respect they deigned to give me had been hard won in battle against the shayde and dresalods. "Not as far as he's concerned."

"His mistake will be his downfall."

"You must not say such a thing," I hissed.

Madr's jaw tightened, and he secured his moss-tinged hair so common in the royal Lumen Clan at the nape of his neck. I'd received my wine-colored streaks from my mother. "I merely state a fact."

"Do not." I shook my head to reinforce my words. "Never."

"My damn father thinks I'm still fifteen. At twenty-eight, I'm perfectly capable of protecting myself." He slapped my arm. "Besides, you might find yourself hunting tonight."

"You know I don't wish to claim a mate."

"You don't want someone to warm your bed and give you orclings?" my fellow Azuris clansman, Viskeete, asked from a branch below me. His husky laugh rang out. "Better chance for us, then."

Others murmured agreement from where they crouched or sat on tree limbs nearby.

The sun would soon set, and two women would leave the village and enter the forest. Eighteen males—three from each of our six orc clans—would hold their breath, waiting to see who would be gifted with a mate.

Seventeen males, actually, because I was here to protect Madr, not chase after a woman.

"I believe you will hunt this night." Speaking as if he could hear my thoughts, Madr hefted his flail. "No one will dare harm me even if you're not standing at my side."

"I'll admit, you're probably better with that weapon than me," I said, noting how the spiked ball on the end of the chain secured to the top of the shaft sparkled in the late-day sunlight.

"*That* has yet to be proven." He braced his palm on my shoulder, staring into my eyes. "Assuming I'm not selected tonight, I'll happily join you on the mats when we return home to prove the point."

I'd gladly fight my half-brother for sport. We'd wrestled and held friendly competitions against each other for much of our lives.

"I'll take you up on that." I kept my voice low so the others wouldn't hear, not that Madr would care. He was the easiest royal to get along with.

"One comes," Fudron of the Basselt Clan said. He lifted his hand, and we all turned to watch a woman wearing a long dress and carrying a bag slip through the large fortress gate. She hurried toward the forest, pausing to glance back only once, before she slipped into the woods below us. Finding a trail, she bunched up her skirts and ran.

"Ah." Fudron's Basselt pendant, a gray circle to represent stone or the very world we lived upon, flared where it dangled on his bare chest. He shot us a tusk-filled grin before springing to the ground and racing after her.

"Seventeen of us left," Madr said, standing. "And only one more female—for this year, that is." He gripped the tree trunk and watched the gate. It swung closed, the bar banging as it was secured.

We watched. We waited.

The sun escaped below the horizon, and guards on the fortress walls lit torches.

When the gate opened once more, we all tensed, even me who did not wish to hunt—*ever*.

A woman dressed in a blue skirt and lighter blue top stumbled out through the opening.

The gate banged shut behind her, and like so many others had in the past—poor frightened creatures that they were—she turned and threw herself at the solid panel.

"Please." Even with the distance between us, I could hear her sobs. "Lyneth. Please let me see Lyneth!"

There was something about her voice . . .

My Azuris Clan pendant, a metal disc made up of swirls coming to spikes that represented waves and bound on a strip of leather around my neck, flared before dimming.

Around me, soft groans of dismay rang out. A few males leaped off the branches and jogged toward the clearing where we'd left our voxes.

"No running for the rest of us tonight," one male said.

"Or rutting," added Viskeete, cupping his groin.

Madr's unusual green eyes echoed their disappointment, but a grin rose on his chiseled face as he smacked my shoulder. "I'm happy for you. Go claim her, brother."

He wasn't upset—not too much. A flaring clan pendant meant your fate had been chosen. No one denied the call.

Just like with all orc males throughout the kingdom, we had few chances to mate with anyone but a human.

Ten years ago, while we battled dresalods on the seashore, some slipped past our defenses and clattered through our city. They found our women hiding in the central compound. Sweeping through it, they killed most of them, my mother and Madr's among them.

To our utter horror, the dresalods ripped through those hiding. We slayed all the attackers, but there was no denying the devastation they'd wrought. Our funeral pyres had scorched the air for almost a week, and the mourning cries echoed in my city to this day.

Our species would die out unless we planted orclings in other females. That was when our gazes turned to the human village being decimated by the land creatures called shaydes.

Per our agreement, we protected the fortress from the shaydes, and they gifted us with two females each year.

"Bring her by the palace to introduce her to me," Madr said with a tusk-filled grin. "In a month or so, when your heat for her has begun to wane."

"Mine never would," another orc said with a snort. "It's said when the fates choose your mate, she'll love you—and ache for you—forever. I'd like some of that."

"As would we all," Madr said ruefully.

"Go," someone shouted at the woman from the top of the wall, drawing my attention that way. "Do your duty to your people!"

When the male threw a bag down at her and it hit her shoulder, a snarl ripped up my throat.

"Lyneth," she cried plaintively before pivoting to face the forest. With the bag clutched in her hand, she stumbled away from the wall, crossing the big open plain. Her nearly white hair streamed behind her, and moonlight gleamed on her medium-toned skin.

"Lovely," Madr said in awe. "The fates have been kind to you, Jaus."

That would be a first.

When the woman stepped onto the narrow forest trail, she lifted her skirts and bolted, running beneath where we perched in the trees high above.

She disappeared into the dense brush.

"Aren't you going after her?" Madr turned my way with his eyes wide with amazement. "She's yours. You must claim her."

So said the fates.

"I don't wish for a mate," I growled with a snap of my tusks. "I'm too busy commanding the army."

"Not all the time."

"My home is small."

Madr smirked. "Your bed is big enough for two."

"He'll be stacked on top of her most of the time anyway," someone else said.

Low laughter rang out, though I doubt the sound reached the forest floor.

"I'll capture her if you don't. Rut her not long after." Viskeete rose to a crouch, his feral gaze locked on where the woman had disappeared into the forest. "I don't need love to plant an orcling in her belly." A female wouldn't fare well under his touch. I'd already caught him kicking a chall. After driving my fist into his tusks, I told him if he did anything like that again, I'd kill him.

I suspected I'd soon have to carry out my threat.

"You will not take her," I snarled, straightening. I slid my mace from the sheath on my back and hefted it.

"In case you didn't know, you don't claim her with *that* weapon," someone said. "Perhaps use the one between your legs?"

"Go." Madr nudged my side. "I promise I won't allow anyone near enough to harm me."

"I cannot leave you." It was my sworn duty for tonight, not chasing after a female I didn't want.

"I also promise I'll fly home with the others," Madr added.

Two of my clansmales pressed their fists against their chests and nodded solemnly.

"See? I'm perfectly safe." The grim look in Madr's eyes told me he'd be safe even if they hadn't volunteered to accompany him back to the castle. His father needed to realize his precious son had grown up into a hardened warrior who was more than capable of handling himself in battle.

My growl ripped out. Duty was my life, but the flare of my pendant told me my wishes meant nothing in this matter.

I cocked my head, making out the subtle pads of her footsteps a clik or so away.

When the cry of a shayde rang out from that direction, my pulse roared. No shayde would harm *my* mate.

"It stalks her," Madr snarled.

I leaped to the ground—a solid, thirty-foot drop, and with my mace lifted, raced after her.

CHAPTER 3
RHOSLYN

With the bag Kael had thrown down clutched in my hand, I stumbled through the forest. Hopefully, the fates would be kind and show me a place where I could hide. So far, I heard no one chasing me, but the orcs may not have arrived in this area yet.

The bag contained clothing. We left two beside the gate on the morning of the hunt. Over the past ten years, the orcs had claimed twenty women from our village. With over a thousand people residing behind the fortress walls, the hunt didn't deplete our numbers by many.

No, it just damned those twenty to a lifetime with an orc.

My lungs raging from running, and with sweat coiling down my spine, I slowed my pace to a walk. If only the moon would rise, then I might be able to see. I peered around, but other than a long berry bramble on my right side I couldn't see through, I hadn't found a place to shelter. Would the orcs find me if I climbed a tree?

If I could wait out the night, they'd return to wherever they came from, and I could make my way home to the fortress. I'd avoid Eamon and be there for my sister like I had been since the shaydes killed our parents seven years ago when I was eighteen. Back then, I'd thought of marrying, but a woman's place was with her husband, and I worried whoever I chose might not accept Lyneth along with me.

I'd scorned all offers until they ceased asking and gave everything I had inside me to my sister. It was worth it.

I didn't need love other than hers.

A subtle sound behind me made my stomach drop to the center of the world. With fear twisting my belly into knots, I peered over my shoulder.

A shayde stood on the path, its red glowing eyes locked on me. Its long, scaled tail whipped back and forth as the creature snarled.

As I pulled my knife, the enormous lizard chittered and rose onto its hind legs, revealing its pale brown, scaled belly. When it thumped back onto all fours, it scrambled toward me, its claws churning up the ground. It would rip me apart in seconds and consume me just as quickly.

With a yelp, I ran down a hill and wove through a

thick stand of trees, hoping it would need to slow its pace to follow.

Few outran a shayde. The memory of what the villagers brought home that day—the only remains of my parents—tracked through me, making my spine spasm. I needed to find a safe spot where I could defend myself; if my puny knife could be considered defense.

Bursting from the thick stand of trees, I raced along a narrow path cutting through deep grass, my ears trained behind me.

This was why two women were sent into the forest each year. They paid the price to keep the shaydes away. The creatures couldn't climb the fortress walls, but they would hunt us relentlessly whenever we ventured outside the enclosure. Only the presence of the orcs kept them away.

My heart on fire, I raced into another patch of woods, my footsteps too loud on the fallen leaves strewn across the path. I struggled to hold on to my knife in my sweaty grip.

The shayde's rank breath raked down my spine, and I whimpered. To think I'd feared becoming an orc's mate only to be shredded by a beast like my parents instead. Poor Lyneth. This wasn't fair to her or me.

Thuds rang out from my right. Another shayde? I'd heard they rarely hunted in packs. Reality and myth were leagues apart, however.

An orc burst from the trees and slammed toward me, a huge mace in his meaty hand. He thrust himself between me and the shayde, a growl ripping up his throat.

While I should keep running—after all, it was the orc's job to protect the village from shaydes—I stopped, pressing my back against a tree as the orc rushed toward the shayde, his mace swinging.

The shayde leaped toward the orc, who moved much quicker than a large male such as him should be able to do. His mace impacted with the shayde's head, driving the beast to the ground.

The shayde twitched and the red glow in its eyes extinguished.

With a grunt, the orc yanked his mace from the dead creature's head. He pivoted toward me, his dark gaze appraising me in a way that made my skin quiver and my heart flounder.

Tightening my grip on my blade, I fled around the tree and ran from this new threat. He came after me, keeping pace much too easily with his long strides.

A glance back showed a scowl creasing his angular face. He coiled a thick finger my way, as if he thought I'd merrily twirl around and race over to him. Leap into his arms and allow him to tumble us to the floor of the forest where he'd claim me.

Why was my skin tingling at the thought?

Adrenaline, that's what it was. I'd almost been killed by the shayde. My skin was aflame from fear, not desire.

And why was the pendant he wore made up of metal swirls glowing where it bounced on his chest?

I didn't pause to gape long, but the impression of him sunk into my mind. Broad chest and huge shoulders. A narrow waist and thick thighs. Greenish-gold skin. He wore only a thick weapon's wrap around his waist that dipped between his legs to barely cover his bulging groin.

His hair appeared streaked with berry, I thought inanely, as I rushed down a hill and slogged up another. By the time I reached the top, the hoarse wheeze of my lungs echoed around me. My heart thundered in my chest as if it planned to break through its cage and run until it reached the end of the world.

He still stalked me, and he'd drawn closer, moving only a footstep or two behind.

He *toyed* with me.

Anger ripped through me, giving me the strength to keep going. I wouldn't easily give into an orc's unbridled lust.

With a grumble, he reached out, grabbing my arm in his meaty paw. He yanked me back against his muscular chest.

I gaped up at his dark eyes, gasping as I took in tusks the size of my thumbs jutting up from his jawline. One and a half times my size, this male towered over me. He'd crush me, destroy me with his claiming.

As I stared at him, unable to breathe, his cock shifted beneath his loincloth and pressed against my spine.

Wrenching free from his grip, I swung out at him

with my knife. It sliced across his abs, though I only delivered a scratch.

Frowning, he looked down at the wound.

Turning, I bolted, whimpers escaping my trembling lips. He was going to kill me now, not claim me as his mate.

Before I could take one step, he tackled me, dragging me down to the ground. He rolled until I lay beneath him. Looming over me, he braced his enormous palms on either side of my shoulders. His glare cut through his chiseled features.

"You attacked me," he said in the universal language.

"You . . ." I couldn't drum up a solid accusation. So far, he'd done nothing other than slay a shayde to keep it from killing me.

And stalk me.

One side of his thick brow lifted sardonically. "If you wish to cause true harm, tiny one, you need to slash harder with your knife."

I flailed at him with my blade, trying to gut him, but he grabbed my wrists and pinned them over my head, tightening until my knife slipped from my grasp. He picked it up and tossed it aside with ease.

"Enough, woman." He smacked his palm on the ground beside my head. His lower body pressed against mine, and something much too large shifted beneath his loincloth.

Twisting, I shrieked, trying to shove him off, but I might as well try to roll a boulder uphill.

He grinned. "You also need to learn how to fight better, tiny one."

"Let me go. Please." I bucked up against him, cringing when my groin impacted with his.

He'd impale me. Split me in two with one thrust. Then leave me whimpering on the forest floor, seeded with his orcling.

"I'm afraid I can't do that," he said blandly.

"Why not?"

"Because I've been forced to claim you."

I blinked slowly at him, unsure what to make of his statement. My fear of another shayde attack faded. If nothing else, this orc would protect me.

"I don't wish for a mate," he added.

"Then don't chase one down and claim her."

His dark gaze met mine, and I found unexpected humor there. "Yet, here I am, doing so."

"You don't need to claim me. I don't want a mate either." I wasn't sure where I found my will to growl at him, but it must've festered inside me like my scorn for Eamon.

"Duly noted." He levered himself up and off me, dragging me from the ground along with him.

Before I could try to break free, he hefted me over his shoulder. I landed with a soft whoof as the wind crushed from my lungs.

With his big hand cupping my ass and my bag in his hand, he took off, running deeper into the woods.

CHAPTER 4
JAUS

I didn't want a mate, but it appeared I had one. At least I'd kept her from being eaten by a shayde.

My Azuris pendant, gifted to me by my clan when I reached maturity fifteen years ago, glowed the moment I saw her. It still glowed, though the light had dimmed. It would blaze once again when I claimed her, then extinguish for the rest of my days.

I didn't want her.

"I have a well-paying position in the kingdom," I growled as I jogged along the trail that would take me to the open meadow where I'd left my vox, Feyla. I'd trained her from the moment she emerged from the seed. Tamed to my touch, she'd wait.

"I'm glad for you," the impertinent female said.

I wasn't mad at her, per se. I was angry with myself for coming here tonight. Irritated with my body's response to her succulent scent. And with my pendant for shouting out to the clans that she was my fated one.

"I'm much too busy for a mate." I rushed down a hill and through the thick stand of trulist trees beyond. "I'm the commander of the forces. I need to spend my days reviewing mission plans. Preparing orders and briefing subordinates. Training in battle." Doing all I could to prove I was worthy.

I hefted my mace to reinforce my point. "I need to spend my nights resting in preparation for the next day's duties, not rutting you."

"When did I ask you to rut me?" she asked, her palms too warm on my back. Each time she slid them across my skin, lust ripped through me.

"You ran through the woods on the night of the hunt."

"If you don't want two of us to leave the fortress and run through the woods at night, don't make that an annual requirement."

"We provide you with protection in exchange for this," I bellowed, frustration and irritation with my situation pouring through me.

"There's no need to snarl."

"I'm speaking in a normal tone. I'm not snarling."

"It sure seems like you are from where I'm . . . lying."

Because her heady scent kept hitting my senses like a club to the side of my skull, I lowered her to the ground, though I kept a tight grip on her wrist. I may not want her, but I wasn't going to allow her to flee.

"Why not let me go if you don't want a mate?" she asked, peering up at me with incredible blue eyes the exact color as my Feyla. Her pale hair was common among her people, though it was the exact opposite of an orc's dark strands woven through with clan colors.

Would our orclings be gifted with her coloring or mine?

A growl shot up my throat, and I stomped along the trail, tugging her with me, though I slowed my pace when I noted she had difficulty keeping up. I didn't want her to fall or scrape her tender skin.

"You're my mate whether I want you or not," I said.

She frowned. "It's not as if we're wedded and everyone's saying you can't divorce me."

"There's no divorce among true mates."

Her lips twisting, she shook her head. "That sounds like a tough situation if the couple doesn't get along."

My footsteps slowed as I approached the meadow where I'd left Feyla. "You'll fall in love with me and be content with what you have. *I'll* be the one finding a way to get along."

She snorted. "Love needs to be earned, and at this rate, I can't ever see *you* earning my love."

I huffed. "Why aren't you afraid of me?"

"It'll take more than an orc dragging me through the forest to spark fear in my heart." She spoke with a lift of her tiny chin, but a subtle tremor came through her voice. "I will say, however, that I'm grateful you don't wish to rut with me."

The problem was, my body did, even if my mind was not in agreement. She was my mate. I would do my duty to produce orclings with her body.

She was winded already. If she were one of my subordinates, I'd make her run for many months until she developed sufficient stamina.

Was that appropriate to ask of a mate?

"I said I don't *wish* to rut with you. That doesn't mean I won't." I paused, peering through the spindly trees toward the meadow. It paid to approach every situation with care, though I doubted Feyla would allow a threat to come near.

"You're saying I must expect you to pounce on me soon."

"Pounce?"

"You know." She waved to my cock straining against the leather of my loincloth. "Impale me with that thing."

"I will not impale *that thing* inside you unless you beg." Which she would do. I didn't take females against their will.

With this female, I sensed persuasion would work well in my favor.

She was my mate even if I didn't want her. I'd claim her despite my interest in setting her aside.

She snorted. "I have no reason to worry then, because I don't plan to beg you to fuck me."

"You issue a challenge I'm more than worthy of."

A soft laugh burst from her.

Turning her to face me, I glared down at her. "Many

wish to rut with me. Kiss me." I wasn't being conceited. They wanted me because I was a male with considerable power, not because they cared one bit for who I was inside.

"I thought all the orc women were dead."

"A few remain."

"And they're universally salivating to get into your loincloth?" The tone of her voice told me she was skeptical, and that irritated me as much as the position I now found myself in.

"They are."

"Well, good for you. You can rut with them instead of me." Peering around, she frowned. "Where are you taking me?"

"To the kingdom."

"Let me go, and I promise I'll keep out of your way so you can keep fucking the females salivating all over your ankles."

"They do not salivate."

"Whimper, then."

I sighed. "They only whimper when I fuck them. Or scream out their joy."

There was no denying the sarcasm in her laugh.

"I meant they seek me figuratively," I conceded.

"Ah, so you've been bragging."

I rolled my eyes, unsure what to make of her impertinence. No orc female spoke to an illustrious male such as me in a tone like this. "You have a sour mouth, mate."

Her grin made my cock twitch. "You're not the first person to tell me that."

"Who has discussed your mouth?" I snarled, ready to kill anyone who so much as looked at her.

"Just a horrible man I'm glad to get rid of. Leave me here, and I'll return to the fortress."

"To the male who discussed your lips?"

"To the one who wants to kiss them, though I've done a decent job of avoiding him thus far."

"How?"

She stiffened. "With my blade that you sadly left behind, plus my ability to impale him in the right place with my knee."

"I'll kill him for touching you." Hefting my mace, I snarled at the area in general.

"I have other options." Her pretty eyes lit up. "There are herbs that will take care of him for me."

"You will not poison *me*."

Her lips quirked up on one side, but she said nothing further.

RHOSLYN

I never thought I'd be having an almost civilized conversation with an orc about fucking.

No woman had ever returned from a hunt to share what happened after they were captured. We assumed they were taken against their will. Never killed because the orcs needed us alive to produce orclings.

Leave it to me to be captured by an orc who didn't want me. It shouldn't make me feel upset. No one other than my sister and a few friends back at the fortress cared if I lived or died, so why should he be any different?

It would be nice to find love and companionship with someone—not this orc, however. He was much too snarly.

And conceited.

"We must go." He tugged me behind him, aiming for a meadow ahead. Something big and pale blue gleamed there in the moonlight, but I couldn't make out what it was.

"What will we do when we reach the kingdom?" I asked, trying not to trip in the dark. The moon may have finally risen, but clouds had cast a caul across her face.

"*You'll* remain in my quarters. *I'll* resume my duties."

"What will *my* duties be since I won't be producing your orclings?"

"You'll wash my clothing. Prepare my meals. Keep my quarters tidy."

"Why not hire someone for that?"

He scowled down at me. "Why would I need to hire someone when I have you?"

Good point.

"And you will help me bathe," he added.

"Groom yourself," I snapped. Why was I picturing this big brawny orc lounging in a tub completely naked? I didn't want to see any part of him, especially his cock.

"I won't need to groom myself now that I have you."

I huffed, unsure what recourse I had. I was completely within his power, and I suspected his people would agree.

"You'll also warm my bed at night." This time, he didn't look my way when he spoke.

"You won't find me willing."

"Believe me, you will be."

Egotistical orc. No. Way.

"I'll try to escape," I said fiercely.

"If you escape, someone else will try to claim you

before you take two steps beyond my door. They won't treat you as gently as me."

"You call throwing me over your shoulder gentle?"

"I could've claimed you when you were pinned beneath me on the forest floor."

"You only didn't because you don't wish to rut with me."

"My pendant has chosen you," he said patiently. "I'll resign myself to it eventually."

"Thanks?" I sighed and walked with him out into the meadow.

An enormous pale blue beast rose onto its haunches, its iridescent wings rippled across its back, its four clawed feet dug into the soil. It arched its long neck, tipping its head toward the sky.

Its roar shook the world around me—and my soul.

Turning its beady eyes my way, it stalked toward me, its feet thundering on the ground.

CHAPTER 6
JAUS

When my new mate gasped and reeled backward, I hefted my mace, scanning the area without finding a threat.

At least my fellow orcs had already departed with their voxes. By the time we reached the kingdom, I expected to find Madr safe behind the castle walls and me relieved of my duty to guard him.

"It's . . . It's a . . ." the female said, backing into the shelter of the woods.

"What's your issue, maiden?" I snarled, glaring around.

"There's a . . . beast!" Her finger lifted, pointing at Feyla.

Not a shayde, then. If they were wise, they'd remain in the shadows. I wasn't the only one who'd quickly dispatch them. Feyla would thunder toward them, her fangs slicing them in half with one bite.

"Come along, tiny mate." I tugged her out into the meadow toward Feyla.

"The beast will eat me!"

Actually, other than the now dead shayde, I was the only beast in the vicinity who wanted to eat her.

No, I did not wish to do that with her, I chided myself. I'd rut with her solely to create orclings and that didn't include sucking on her clit. I'd ensure she found pleasure in the main act, but doing more than that could risk everything I'd worked so hard for since my mother was kicked out of my father's house when I was young.

"Feyla won't harm you." Keeping a tight grip on the woman's wrist, I tugged her toward my vox who'd patiently awaited my return.

"It's . . . enormous," she gulped.

"How else do you expect it to carry an orc?"

She shook her head. "I don't . . . I didn't know something like this existed, so how could I think anything about it?"

I couldn't imagine how she or her people had not seen even one vox. They were our primary means of traveling great distances.

We walked over to Feyla's side, and she turned her long snout our way, studying the woman.

"She's mine," I snarled, tapping the end of Feyla's snout. "Don't eat her."

Feyla huffed and turned back to face forward.

The female kept her wide-eyed gaze on my vox.

One heft, and I'd tossed her up onto the beast's

scaled back. She floundered, her legs settling around the base of Feyla's neck, her hands lifting as if she didn't dare touch the beast.

This female was wiser than she'd first appeared.

After looping the tie of her bag over one of Feyla's neck spikes, I leaped up behind the woman, settling her body against mine. My mate fit well there for such a tiny being.

My infernal cock noted her closeness and started stiffening. Even my growl wouldn't make it stop.

"I'm Jaus Kreedaull. What's your name, female?" I asked as I nudged my heels into Feyla's sides, urging her to take flight. If I focused on guiding my vox, my cock might settle down and behave.

Feyla burst off the ground, her wings snapping out to catch air and lift us higher. A few flaps, and we soared above the forest, heading toward the kingdom far enough in the distance that we wouldn't see it for a very long time.

"Ahh," the female cried, her hands fluttering. She scrambled around to face me, clinging to my chest, her legs wrapping around me.

With her legs spread like that, her skirt hitched up, revealing creamy thighs I ached to sink my fingertips into. This position also hinted at the juncture between her legs where I wanted to bury my face and lick and suck until she shrieked out her pleasure.

My damn cock ripped up inside my loincloth, struggling to break free.

"Stop moving," I snapped.

She looked up at me, her lush lips parting. Damn kissable lips. My pendant flared again, lighting up like a star. If the shaydes could fly, they'd spike toward us to tear us asunder.

She sucked in little breaths, and I suspected she'd make the same sound while I drilled my cock inside her.

"I doubt *ahhh* is your name," I said dryly, wrapping my arm around her to keep her from sliding off Feyla. I didn't like how much I enjoyed holding her snugly against my chest.

"It . . . It . . .!" She pinched her lips closed and swallowed hard.

"If I'd known I could shut you up just by showing you to Feyla, I would've done it a lot sooner."

She stiffened. "It's normal to be frightened of a beast such as this. Flying! I can't believe it. We're flying. And my name's Rhoslyn."

The smile she shot me made my lungs seize and my pendant sparkle.

"Bright, isn't it?" she asked, frowning at it hanging on my chest.

I clutched the pendant, blocking the light. "This is a symbol of the Azuris Clan. It represents water."

"Why does it keep flaring?"

Because she was my fated one. It blazed only for her.

"It means nothing," I said.

"I see." She frowned up at me and snuggled against my chest. "I'm not so frightened any longer."

"Why not?" As far as I could see, nothing had changed.

"Because . . ." She pinched her eyes shut before she looked up at me. "Despite not wanting me as your mate or wishing to fuck me, you've proven you'll protect me. If nothing else, I know you'll keep me from falling."

I suspected resisting pretty little Rhoslyn was going to be harder than singlehandedly fighting off an entire legion of dresalods.

CHAPTER 7
RHOSLYN

We flew through the night, but still didn't reach the end of the forest.

"It goes on forever," I said, too tired to engage in a battle of wits with Jaus any longer.

"I'll stop and you can rest."

"No fucking," I warned.

He snorted but said nothing.

Feyla soared lower, her claws skimming across the tops of the trees. When an open area loomed ahead, she dropped down so fast, my belly wasn't sure it could keep up. I gulped and swallowed as the giant creature landed with a dull thud on thick, overgrown grass.

Before I could say a peep, Jaus wrapped his arm around my waist and leaped off the vox, taking me with him. He placed me on the ground and removed my bag, handing it to me. I dropped it on the grass, too tired to care what might be inside.

Jaus also unhooked a small pouch from one of the spikes strutting down the beast's neck. From it, he pulled a flask and handed it to me. "Drink. I'll light a fire. We'll sleep here for the rest of the night and continue traveling tomorrow."

"How much farther?"

"We'll reach the city late tomorrow afternoon."

"So far." If I escaped, I'd never be able to walk back to the village. My heart plunged down into my belly, the two churning together. Tears smarted in my eyes, but I sniffed them away. I was here so Lyneth wouldn't be, and I'd thank the fates for that.

Jaus gathered wood and cleared an area beneath the broad branches of an evergreen. He lit a fire quickly and the heavy scent of smoke clogged my nose when it gusted my way.

"Sit," he said, waving to a spot beside him.

I still stood where he'd left me beside Feyla. She watched me with what I swore was indulgence in her eyes. At least she hadn't taken a bite out of my arm.

With a huff, she started nibbling on the grass by her front feet.

"She doesn't eat meat," Jaus said, tossing a few thick branches onto the fire.

After drinking from the flask, I walked over and dropped it beside him. "I need to . . ."

He nodded and rose from a crouch, hefting his mace. "I'll go with you."

A squirm rippled through me. "Please, no."

"I promise not to watch."

Because he snarled out the words, I decided to trust him in this at least. Pivoting, I walked into the woods, though I didn't go far. The sound of the shayde's shriek still haunted my mind, and I didn't want to draw another close. We needed to rest, not fight them off for the rest of the night.

After I'd finished, we returned to the fire.

Jaus crouched again, adding more wood. I sat opposite him, savoring the warmth of the flames licking hungrily at the logs.

Rising, he came around and dropped down beside me, placing the pouch in his lap. Before I could move again, he latched onto my arm. "You'll remain with me, tiny mate, to make sure nothing snatches you away."

Shivers tracked through me. I peered into the woods, but all I could see were the flames I'd just stared into.

"Don't look at them directly. They'll momentarily blind you, and you won't know something's stalking you until it . . ." His low chuckle rang out. "Pounces."

"Wise advice I'll apply to you as well."

His chuckle grew louder. After placing his mace in the sheath on his back, he opened the pouch and drew out an oil-soaked cloth, unwrapping it to reveal large chunks of what looked like grain, dried berries, and something greasy holding it all together. He broke one in half and handed me a piece, sinking his tusks into the other eagerly.

I nibbled on it, and my belly soon roared, stating tiny

bites were not enough. After eating more than half, however, I handed the rest to him.

"You need it," he said. "How else will you grow my orclings in your nicely rounded belly?"

"It'll be interesting to see how you intend to gain orclings from me if you don't plan to fuck me."

"Oh, I'll rut you soon enough."

"Allow me to say I don't look forward to that moment."

"You will."

"Bragging *again*?"

"Stating the truth." He ate the rest of the meal and tossed the pouch over to where I'd left the water flask. "Time to sleep, tiny mate."

"I'll lay there." I pointed to the other side of the fire. "And you can remain over here."

"We'll sleep together from now on."

My breath caught, but I bit back my sharp retort. I was too tired to keep up the battle. I could lift my sword, so to speak, again in the morning.

He laid down, tugging me along with him, keeping me between him and the fire.

"You don't need to stand watch?" I asked softly.

"Feyla will do that for me. She'll hear shaydes coming closer before I will, and she'll attack while sounding the alarm." One of his arms curled up near the hilt of his mace and the other remained snug around me. "Sleep, mate. I'll rouse you in the morning."

"I wake up early already." At dawn, most days.

Between brewing tinctures and potions and tending to those in need of my healing skills, my day was full. I wasn't the only healer in the village, but even without bragging, I could easily state I was better than most. My fellow villagers would suffer with me gone.

Eamon was an incredibly stupid mayor for not seeing my worth outside of warming his bed.

Jaus tugged me tight against his length. I'd protest our closeness if I wasn't savoring his warmth. This male was a second fire, and it wasn't long before my eyelids started sinking from exhaustion.

His cock prodded my ass but for now, I'd trust him not to stuff it inside me.

CHAPTER 8
RHOSLYN

I woke to Jaus smacking my ass. "Get up, tiny mate. No more slumbering by the fire for you. It's well past time for us to leave."

Sitting up, I peered around, noting Feyla chewing grass as she stood in the center of the meadow, her spiked tail sweeping back and forth slowly, and her intent gaze scanning the surrounding forest.

I turned my attention to Jaus.

"Damn," I said. "I was praying you were a nightmare who'd flee before morning." I shoved my hair out of my eyes and tidied it in a hasty braid. My bladder protested the movement, and I dreaded telling him I needed to enter the woods once more. Last night, it was dark. Now, he'd be able to see everything.

Jaus's lips split in a big grin as he watched me fix my hair, his strong tusks gleaming brightly in the sunlight.

"I'm your fondest dream, tiny mate, never your nightmare."

"For a male who doesn't want me, you sure keep suggesting you do."

"Rutting is one thing. Wanting is another."

I huffed. "It works both ways."

"For now."

Rising, I started toward the woods. "Are you suggesting you're going to fall in love with me and beg me to return your affection?"

"I'm not concerned in the least about that."

"What does that mean?" I paused while I decided how best to avoid a big cluster of brambles ahead.

He lifted me up and dropped me on the opposite side. He was handy for that at least.

I walked a bit farther with him right behind me, his hand on the hilt of his mace.

"I won't fall in love," he said. "But you will. You'll succumb like every other female claimed during the hunt."

I huffed. "I hold my heart, and I don't easily give it away."

"As do I. But it's common for those fated to orcs to love their new mates fiercely and quickly."

"I'll prove that notion wrong." I sent him a scowl. "Turn, please."

He rolled his eyes but did so.

After I was finished, we returned to the now dead fire and Feyla waiting.

"Back up on my vox, tiny mate," he said, swinging me up easily, positioning me to face Feyla's tail. One leap, and he sat with me, tugging me up onto his lap. Now my legs had no place to go but around his hips. His arm encircled my waist, and his feet moved subtly beneath us.

Feyla jumped up, her wings snapping out, and we were soon soaring above the forest again.

We flew in silence, which was a welcome respite from his bragging and my snapping. I wasn't normally the type to squabble—other than with Eamon, and with him, I only felt dismay, not desire.

Horror dumped through me when I realized something. Despite our ongoing arguments, I was attracted to Jaus.

I do not desire him.

Yet I was haunted by his certainty that all fated mates fell for their orc husbands.

We stopped twice to eat more of the packed berries, seeds, and nuts, and drain the rest of the water.

All the time we flew, Jaus intently scanned the area around us, his gaze always returning to my face. At least his eyes didn't drop from there, his hand following. I could be grateful for that.

He'd made it clear I'd lie beside him, but for now, he didn't appear ready to give reign to his threat to mate with me.

By the time the sun tiptoed down toward the horizon, we were approaching the orc city. A vast body of water gleamed pale lavender beyond the outer walls with only a few crests of white breaking the glassy surface.

"I've never seen anything like it before," I said in awe. "It's . . ."

"What do you speak of?" His brow narrowed as he scanned the area. Did he think we'd be attacked? Who'd dare come near Feyla, let alone the magnificent orc riding her with a weapon half my size strapped to his back? Yesterday, he'd embedded the head of it in the shayde with an ease that stunned me.

"I speak of the enormous body of water," I said.

"It's the Tartledge Sea. Don't go there."

"Why not?"

"Though I plan to keep a tight rein, you'll have free time," he said sharply. "Do not go near the sea."

"You need to tell me why."

"The dresalods will see you."

"I don't know what they are."

"Let's hope you never find out."

I shivered, though I wasn't sure why.

"Your city's gorgeous." As Feyla flew closer, I took in the sunlight glinting off buildings that appeared crafted from the finest silver. "We build wooden structures, as you probably know."

"They burn. Silver doesn't as easily."

"While it's good to avoid burnable material, why do you feel the need to build all your homes from metal?"

"There was a time when voxes like my Feyla

attacked." He patted her leathery hide, and she grunted, soaring down toward the big city. "An earlier species of voxes could light an entire building aflame with one blast of its lungs."

"Feyla can't?"

"It was bred out of them ages ago."

I couldn't imagine how horrible it must've been when they'd swoop over a village, burning everything in sight.

"We train them from the time they slip from their seed," he added. "And continue to breed only those who don't possess fire."

"You own all of them?"

"No one owns a vox. They allow us to work with them. A few untrained beasts exist, but we've driven them far enough away they no longer seek us."

A chill ripped through me. When I'd remained behind the fortress walls, I'd felt safe. Back then, I thought the only threat came from shaydes. Now I'd discovered I lived in an incredibly dangerous world.

"I thought orcs lived a relaxed life other than the rare time you have to drive shaydes away from the fortress," I said.

"That's only one of the small tasks we engage in."

The sun had risen enough in the sky to disperse the shadows curling along the sides of buildings. As Feyla swooped above the rooflines, her shadow chased us through the cobblestone streets below. A few orcs paused and looked up. Some waved.

"So many houses," I said. "How many orcs live here?"

"Thousands, plus a few tiny women like you."

I snorted. Most considered me tall and extra curvy. "I'm not tiny."

"You are to me."

"Strength doesn't come only from muscle in case you didn't know."

"I wouldn't be much of a military commander if I didn't realize that already."

He kept staring at me, and I wondered what he thought—other than believing me tiny.

"Do all the women taken during the past ten hunts live here?"

"Here or with other orc clans. They're happily mated to their orc husbands."

My belly coiled tight. When we reached his home, would he claim me fully? I wasn't sure why, but the prospect made tingles spread through my body. Would I have the will to fight him off?

"They were *forced* to mate with orcs," I pointed out.

One side of his thick brow rose. "Like I've forced you to mate?"

"You said I'll sleep in your bed, that you'll soon fuck me."

"Not until you beg."

I was beginning to suspect it wouldn't take much for me to do so.

My cheeks stung with embarrassment. He'd made it clear he didn't find me desirable. I should be grateful he only wanted a servant and someone to warm his bed. I could hold back my heart if he didn't make an effort to woo me.

"You know I won't beg." My bravado spoke when I wasn't sure *I* could.

He leaned close to my ear, his eyes alight with humor, and one side of his seductive mouth curved up. "I've barely touched you. You'll soon see."

My skin flamed, and I'd like to say it was still only due to embarrassment, but he smelled too good. And his thick, greenish-golden orc skin felt too good beneath my palms.

"I'm only clinging because I don't want to fall," I said, lifting my chin.

"No other reason, tiny one?"

I wouldn't allow him to irritate me. If any taunting was going to be done, it would come from me, not him. The best way to handle a male like this would be to ignore him—something I was finding a challenge while pressed tightly against his chest.

His cock shifted. He watched me through hooded eyes, but I didn't know what he saw other than a weak, *tiny* human woman. "Your fellow villagers are happy living with their orc mates. Each was more than willing to join with him. They've given birth to orclings, as they should."

There he went again, poking me with his words and the torturous light dancing in his dark eyes.

"*If* I become your mate . . ." I would do all I could not

to succumb to his touch. "You'll end up having orclings with me."

He shrugged, directing his attention ahead. "You're correct."

"Make sure you remember to breathe."

His sharp gaze landed on my face once more. "Why?"

I slipped one of his knives from a sheath at his side and brandished it near his nose. "If you hold your breath, waiting for me to give in, you'll pass out."

"I *never* pass out."

Some did. "Anyway. Don't think I'll be easy to win or plant orclings in."

His laugh burst from his lungs, full and throaty. His hand snapped out, stealing the knife from me with ease. He returned it to the sheath.

"I hate you."

He just snorted, and that irksome, knowing look remained in his eyes. "For now."

How could he be so sure I'd love him?

"I've never craved sex, and I certainly won't with you," I snapped.

"You will."

Argh! I wanted to smack him, but I didn't quite dare. First, I was a healer, not one who dispensed harm.

Second, he was an orc, a fearsome, raging beast according to human legends.

Third, he was very good with his mace.

Although I'd seen nothing beastly about him. He'd killed the shayde, but who wouldn't? Eat or be eaten, and shaydes loved our flesh. Still, he must be beastly inside. And extra snarly.

Jaus was so easily irritated, it was fun to poke him. I'd never learned to control my mouth, and I wasn't about to start now.

"As for my strength, I'll soon surprise you. Mine is inside." I looked up at him, studying him like he did me. I'd seen a few orcs when they came near the fortress, hunting shaydes or discussing the change of guard with those working along the fortress fence. But they always came at night. I'd never had the chance to view one of them up close and in broad daylight.

Jaus's windblown hair hung past his shoulders in a wild disarray, and it was softer than the finest silk. I'd discovered this when Feyla banked to the right sharply to avoid a flock of birds, and I clutched Jaus's shoulders.

What would it be like to run my fingers through it, to kiss along his jawline until I could bury my face in the thick strands?

Kissing him was a foreign concept. I'd never thought of orcs as attractive. They were the stuff of nightmares.

Sadly enough, it wasn't hard for me to feel desire for this devastatingly handsome orc. If I didn't take care, he could be my downfall. He'd made it clear he didn't want me, that he never would.

My heart pinched at the thought. I didn't want *him*. I should be grateful he wouldn't force me.

I was not a true maiden, though he'd called me that earlier. Before my parents died and I had dedicated myself to my sister, I'd been with a man, one I thought I might wed. He asked another when I gently nudged him away.

Sex wasn't anything to ache for, however, at least not with the man I thought I might marry.

With Jaus? Hopefully I could hold on to my will and resist him.

Feyla flew lower, so close to the buildings, her claws could brush across the sharply peaked roofs. Unadorned, the walls of the single and even three-story homes appeared incredibly smooth. If a ferocious creature tried to scale them, their claws would not find purchase. The attacker would slide down the surface and land hard on the ground.

With a subtle nudge of his heel, Jaus directed Feyla to the right. If I wasn't sitting in his lap, I'd miss how carefully he controlled her with a series of complex foot commands.

"I know nothing about voxes," I whispered, though no one could hear but us. A few mounted voxes flying along the coastline were the only other beings in sight.

"You'll learn."

Feyla swept even lower, flying at an angle above the polished cobbled streets weaving among the buildings. We passed a big open market full of orcs hawking their wares, but I didn't see a single woman. Were they kept hidden inside?

We soared toward a tall building nestled among those closest to the coast. Beyond a high, thick wall mounted with bristling guards, I spied a wide strip of black sand patrolled by more orcs wearing heavy armor and carrying numerous weapons. I saw no boats. Who'd dare attack such a formidable force by sea?

At Jaus's command, Feyla dove toward the last building at the end of the long row of them standing high enough to view the sea from the top floor. The vox approached the tower residence at a speed that made my heart roar up into my throat.

I clutched Jaus's arms to the point my fingers must pinch, but he didn't appear to notice.

His flinty gaze remained on the water beyond the high wall encircling the city. Like everything else we'd flown over, the wall was constructed of glassy silver, and it was nearly as tall as the highest buildings.

One of the orcs stalking along the wall paused and released a guttural cry. His arm lifted, pointing toward the water.

Jaus subtly stiffened. If I wasn't pressed against him, I would've missed it. His pulse ticked in his temple, and his lips tightened.

The orc's cry was picked up by those on the shore. They hefted their weapons and pivoted to face the sea in one long line.

Feyla landed on an open, circular area mounted near the roofline of a building, coming to rest with a thud that jarred through my bones. From here, I couldn't make out the wall or the sea.

Shouts and guttural cries echoed from that area, the

voices making the air thicken with tension. This wasn't a welcoming cry. No, if I guessed correctly, they were anticipating battle. From whom?

Jaus leaped off Feyla and reached up, his long fingers encircling my waist easily. I was no tiny maiden despite him calling me that. He lowered me to the smooth stone surface. Before I could speak, he jumped back up onto Feyla's back.

Horns sounded along the wall and shore, discordant and shrill, making my ears ache.

"Get inside," Jaus barked, his gaze feral. After tossing my pitiful bag of possessions onto the stone beside me, he whipped his hand toward a metal door mounted on the side of the tower. A flag with the Azuris symbol fluttered frantically in the breeze at the peak above it.

"Where are we?" I called out over the cries of orcs and something else I'd never heard before in my life. A nightmare had come to life. Shrieks and the sound of claws scrambling for purchase on smooth metal grated across my bones.

"This building is my home," Jaus said.

"You're not coming inside with me?"

He jerked his head back and forth, his gaze fixed on the sea.

A large group of voxes flew over us, the agitated gust from their wings blasting around me.

A growl ripped up Jaus's throat. "I don't have time for this. Get inside!"

He didn't have time for *me*, he meant. It wasn't like I

expected a grand tour of his residence, but I didn't think he'd abandon me the moment we arrived.

"You're going to fuck someone else already?" I gasped the second the words burst from me, dismayed that I'd actually spoken them aloud.

His eyes shuttered.

"Get inside," he said softly. "Please."

My face heated to the point of boiling, and I chided myself for behaving like a fool. He'd been clear about his needs. While I shrieked at him like a harpy, he continued to treat me as he'd stated—gently.

Jealousy coated my throat, sour and sticky, and I swallowed it down, determined to never allow the feeling to rise within me again. It was ridiculous to suspect something like this. It was clear from the cries on the beach that something was attacking the city, that he had to leave to meet the threat with his weapon drawn.

Feyla snapped her teeth, but she didn't appear to send her anger toward me. No, it was also directed at the enormous body of water beyond the wall.

"What's going on?" I asked as Jaus tapped Feyla's sides. "I'll go inside, but please, tell me."

Feyla sprang upward, her wings snapping out to catch the wind.

Another fleet of voxes swooped overhead, the orcs mounted on their spines hefting weapons.

Jaus's gaze met mine, and again, they softened. "Please, Rhoslyn. Get inside. The dresalods are attacking."

CHAPTER 9
JAUS

I couldn't wait much longer. My fellow orcs needed me to command, not just battle beside them.

Shrieks from dying dresalods echoed around us, but the scrapes of many claws on the outer walls told me a large legion had chosen this moment to attack the city. If we didn't drive them back into the water, they'd scale the walls and overrun the streets.

They'd decimate everything and everyone in their path, like they did whenever they left the sea.

If they got past the wall, we'd have to track them one by one, and they'd kill many before we'd defeated them. They bred like ribbers. Even worse, they matured within a few months.

Dreading the sunlight, they used to only attack at night, but they'd become bold over the past year. Now they attacked both day and night.

Despite my need to leave, I kept Feyla hovering above

Rhoslyn, the female I was bound to for the rest of my days. The mate chosen for me by the heart of my clan. The woman I could seduce and plant orclings in soon.

Fuck, did I desire her like no other.

She watched me with an expression I couldn't read, her glorious hair swirling around her like strands of a golden banner. I wanted to mark her as mine. I *craved* her.

My sigh leaked from my tight chest.

"What are dresalods?" Rhoslyn cried, backing toward the door.

Good. She needed to get inside. I needed to leave.

Still, I lingered. I couldn't drag my gaze away.

"They attack. They kill," I snarled. "Unless we eliminate them first."

Her eyes widened with panic, and she whipped her gaze around as if the dresalods perched at the top of the wall, salivating as they leaped toward my home to attack her.

I shouldn't have to explain myself to this tiny female who'd already proven she was anything but weak. I saw her strength in the tilt of her head. I felt it in the way she spoke, unafraid when confronted by a hardened orc commander.

The knowledge that she had a will as taut as mine was already embedded in my heart.

No, *not* my heart. I would take her body willingly, but I would not love her.

"I need to go," I growled.

Her shoulders dropped. "I'm sorry. I'll go inside." Clutching the bag she'd brought with her, she grappled with the door latch behind her, opening it. She stepped into the darkness.

Even now, I did not leave.

She gave me a curt nod. "Help the others. I'll find my way around inside."

Very well.

The hilt of my mace tight in my hand, I urged Feyla toward the sea and the ongoing battle. It was time to reduce the dresalod population if for only a brief time. Show them they were foolish to creep from the sea.

Rhoslyn called to me as Feyla swooped down toward a dresalod hefting itself up onto the top of the wall.

"Come back," she cried.

Did she say this because she feared being alone in the orc city? She must.

The words didn't express growing feelings.

CHAPTER 10
RHOSLYN

After slamming the metal door closed, I slid the thick bar across it. Backing away, I clutched my trembling hands to my throat.

I didn't care if something happened to him—so I told myself.

If he was dead, I might be allowed to return to my beloved sister.

When I slumped against the cold stone wall, I wasn't giving into the conflicted emotions churning inside me.

I didn't *like* Jaus. He irritated me. Taunted me.

He stirred emotions inside me I'd never felt before.

"You just met him a few days ago," I told myself, my whisper as harsh as the cries of death echoing outside. "Remain pleasant and maybe he'll release you from this farce of a mating."

The shrieks grew in volume, and my heart stopped. Was he injured already?

I kept picturing how Jaus had killed the shayde so quickly. He was a commander. Surely that meant he'd return to me safely.

Return to me? Thoughts like that sounded too close to caring, and I didn't like it one bit.

"He's not going to be a true mate to me." Jeez, I didn't even *want* to lie beneath him while he rutted. He was snarly and gruff. How could I ever find that attractive?

My throbbing body told me I just might.

"Forget about him." Stiffening my spine, I bumped off the wall. With my bag in hand, I pivoted and walked farther into the darkness. A light bloomed ahead at the end of the hall, outlined by a whisp lantern hanging beside yet another metal panel. Since the whisp's pace had slowed, I opened the clear front panel and blew on the mechanism inside. It spun faster, and the light brightened.

"Why a second door?" I asked myself. Did Jaus expect the dresalods to breach the outer one?

The shiver tracking through me told me he might.

"Why haven't we heard of the dresalods?" I asked no one.

Perhaps because we were too busy fighting off shaydes to expect anything else. Or they didn't leave this area. Jaus said they came from the sea to attack. They may not be able to remain out of the water for long to cross the forest, though the thought was purely speculation on my part. I'd ask him about them later, when he returned.

If he returned.

"Don't tangle yourself up in fear for him. If he doesn't come back, if he's . . . killed, you can beg whoever's in charge to take you back to the village." With a slight plan in place, my tension eased a fraction.

I released the latch on the door and swung it open, heavy thing that it was. Light for an orc, I bet.

Inside, I shut and barred the second door. How would Jaus get inside?

He could knock.

Ha. If he did so, I might let him in, or maybe I wouldn't. If letting him in gave him the chance to make demands on my body and time, leaving him outside would be my best option. He could sleep on the open balcony or with Feyla. She must have a nest somewhere nearby, and he could snuggle up to her instead of me.

My grin widened as I took in the large living area with windows spaced evenly around the entire outside wall. The room appeared to take up the entire level of the tower. The stairs on the opposite side went down as well as up.

Time to explore.

I trod across the room, tossing my bag onto an orc sized sofa, and paused beside the spiral staircase. "Up or down?"

Why not both?

I climbed and found myself in another large room, this one holding a huge stone structure in the center with piping shooting down from above. I peered inside.

"A tub." Flat stones had been placed around the outer wall at various levels, and a drain in the middle must allow the tub to be emptied through piping above the living area ceiling and the wooden floor beneath my feet. A sink and what I took for a toilet, though we only had dug outhouses back at the village, had been placed on one side of the room. Another large stone tub near the toilet appeared to be for washing clothing, if the wooden racks leaning against the wall beside it were any indication.

Washing my things in a basin would be better than hauling dirty clothing down to the river and cleaning them there, then hauling them back to hang beside the woodstove.

I climbed the staircase to the top and final level, finding a bedroom with an enormous bed neatly made up with thick blankets. Semi-clear panels overhead let in muted sunlight. If I laid on that surface at night, would I be able to see the stars?

"You're going to do all you can to avoid laying on that surface," I told myself. "Laying there will mean sleeping with Jaus, and that could lead to him doing things that could make you beg for more." There had to be another bed here somewhere.

A large group of mounted voxes flew overhead, the sweep of their wings creating a heavy whoosh, and from the shrieks coming from the seaside of the kingdom, they still waged a battle with the dresalods.

Worry for Jaus clouded my mind, but I shoved the

feeling away. I barely knew him. I didn't care for him in that way. It was only my sense of self-preservation gripping my heart, insisting I needed him in order to survive here.

Because I wanted a distraction and I was nosy, I strode over to a large wardrobe and tugged the panels opened, revealing neat rows of clothing, everything from formal tunics with patch medals to simple things like pants and soft shirts. The green tunics would look amazing on Jaus with his greenish-golden skin. And I could only imagine how the pants would hug his thighs and his—

What was I thinking? No matter what he wore, he'd remain an orc. Not despised by my people necessarily, because we needed their protection, but not welcome inside the fortress walls for a social visit.

The thought hit me in the chest like a fist, though I wasn't sure why. Orcs had never given any indication they wished to be welcome in our village.

The bureau drawers held stacks of loincloths made of various materials, though the colors only ranged from tan to brown and gray. Simple things he could wrap around his waist and tuck between his legs to cover his groin. Each had sheaths to hold small weapons. But then, he was a warrior. What else would he wear when he trained? Thick clothing could trip you up and once tripped, it would be over.

The only item on the top of the smooth wooden surface was a simple woven bracelet, too small for Jaus's thick wrist. The intricate braid included pale blue stone beads, and they glinted in the muted sunlight. From the way the weave twisted, I suspected it was old, at least five or more years.

And the slice along each end told me it had been cut from the wearer's wrist.

"Who do you belong to?" I asked it, suspecting its ownership would remain a mystery.

I left his bedroom and took the stairs down to the lowest level, finding a kitchen and dining area, plus a big office with a desk fit for an orc commander. Like with his living area and bedroom, each room was spotlessly clean, and I wondered who'd made sure not a speck of dust or dirt could be found on any surface.

Without outer windows, it was quiet in the kitchen. I raided the cool box and quickly ate the cheese and coarse bread I found at the table, my chin barely reaching the surface when I sat in one of the four chairs. I'd have to sit on a pillow next time or I'd feel comically small.

Belly subdued, I leaned back in the chair and fretted.

"I'm worried about Jaus just like I would be for anyone battling scary creatures," I said. "This has nothing to do with him in particular."

I left the kitchen and went up one level to the living area, sitting on the sofa for what felt like hours, covering my ears to block out the terrifying sounds outside. My breathing echoed in my head, and the rapid drum of my pulse made me ache to find my way to the edge of the city where I could run into the forest forever.

Actually . . .

Rising, I grabbed my bag and scurried over to the door and pressed my ear against it, listening but hearing nothing. I shifted the bar to the side and cracked the panel a fraction. Still silence. Opening the door wider, I hurried down the hall to the outer door, unbarring it as well.

When I opened it a hair and heard nothing, I scooted out through the narrow opening and pressed my back against the tower wall.

The world had gone crazy.

Mounted voxes soared overhead, darting toward the sea. Cries of anger and pain whipped me from every direction, punctuated by ear-piercing shrieks that must be the dresalods.

Dropping my bag, I inched over to the edge of the deck and gripped the half wall so hard, the stone dug into my palms. From here and beyond the high wall, I could see a strip of sandy shore where it met the sea.

Creatures as tall as an orc, with six legs with spiked claws at the tips, scrambled toward orcs slicing out at them with enormous weapons. The creatures' broad, thick shells were flat across their backs, and their larger enormous front claws clicked as they snatched up orcs and flung them into the sea where their brethren waited to drag them down beneath the churning waves.

Orcs attacked them on foot and from the backs of voxes, killing one after another, but they kept coming, a never-ending army from the sea.

I'd never seen anything as bloody and devastating as this battle.

Grunts and cries of pain rang out, the sounds ripping through me like the sharpest stone. Jaus was out there somewhere, struggling to fight off the dresalods. Doing all he could to survive.

Or he could be dead already.

The thought made my heart seize. I pinched my eyes closed, but all I could see was him lying on the sand, blood pouring from numerous wounds, an enormous dresalod ripping him apart with its claws.

"Going somewhere, tiny mate?" Jaus asked from behind me.

Gasping, I spun.

My foot caught on something, and I tumbled over the wall.

CHAPTER 11

JAUS

I grabbed Rhoslyn's arm and lifted her back up to the balcony. Rather than place her on her feet, I held her, savoring the feel of her sweet, lush form, her warmth, and the way she clung to my shoulders.

She soothed the beast still raging inside me, making it huff and back away.

"I told you to remain inside," I said.

I was weary from battling. Weary of killing. But what choice did I have? If we didn't eliminate the threat each time, it would eliminate us.

Her hands fluttered across my chest. "You . . . You're alive."

"Did you wish me dead?"

She looked up sharply. "Should I? I wondered about what they'd do with me if you didn't return."

"Did you think they'd send you back?"

The way her eyes lit up told me more than I wanted

to know. She still wished to return to her village. Why would she not? I'd done nothing to convince her she wanted to be by my side.

Life was such a fragile thing. It could be stolen with one blow of a claw.

"Did it occur to you that they might give you to someone else?" I asked.

She sucked in a breath and pressed her face close to my chest. "At least then, I wouldn't be with you."

She sounded much too happy about the notion.

"Women are rare here and humans have proven they can birth our orclings," I pointed out.

"They can be *forced* to birth your orclings, you mean."

My sigh shot out, and I tightened my jaw. I'd left the fighting, yet I hadn't. Why should I expect anything else from my pretty mate?

"Where's Feyla?" She peered around.

"Flown to her roost."

"You're not battling any longer."

"It's nearly over. See?" I took her over to the wall, and we watched as the last dresalods scurried back into the sea, their spiked claws digging into the soft sand. Their broad, thick shells shifted as they moved, their enormous front claws clicking. One snap could sever an orc's head or a limb from his body.

Our funeral pyres would blaze tonight. How long before there weren't enough of us left to fight off the next wave or the legion after that?

"They look ferocious. They're almost as big as an

orc," she said. "I once read a journal from someone who visited the sea. She called something like this a crab, though in her journal, she indicated crabs were the size of her fist, nothing this large."

"I've never heard the term crab."

"I'm not sure I believe she ever saw them. She was a fanciful person and often told tales of creatures called starfish and of maidens who could lure sailors to their death in the sea. Before she died, she gave me her journal full of stories. I lost it after my parents died."

"Did her tales share a way to defeat the dresalods forever?"

"The stories don't do more than mention them, and I doubt they're much like the beasts who just attacked the city."

"Too bad. It would be nice to find a simple solution."

A shudder ripped through her, and I tightened my hold, showing her that she was safe—for now. "Will they come back?"

"Not for a few months. Their next attack will come once they've added adult creatures to their legions." Or when hunger overwhelmed them.

"I'm glad you survived." Her words whispered across my skin; so soft, I barely heard them. Her hands spread wide on my chest. Like I'd been struck by lightning, electricity jolted through me. My pendant flared before dampening, reminding me she was my fated one.

"Thank you."

She shot me a true smile, and it made me want to

take her to my bed and curl my body around hers. Stroke her. Kiss her.

Taste her.

"Did you find something to eat?" I asked as I strode inside. Holding her with one arm, her bag hooked over the other, I barred the door and continued into my quarters. After tossing her bag onto a chair and hanging my cleaned mace on the hook mounted on the wall, I sat on the sofa and held her, savoring how well she fit in my arms.

Just as I'd grown tired of fighting dresalods, I was weary of battling with my tiny mate.

"Please know that no woman has been forced to have orclings with any of my kind," I said.

"I believe you. I spoke in anger. I'm sorry." She looked up at me, and she didn't struggle to break free. What would it be like to have this female want me? Not because I'd clothe and feed her but have her want *me*, Jaus, the hardened commander who sometimes wished to let down his guard and speak from his heart?

As I'd fought off one dresalod after another, killing or driving them back into the sea, I kept thinking about what might happen to Rhoslyn if I died.

I'd held myself back from others for many years, fearing if I gave myself like my mother had to my father, I could also be hurt.

With each dead dresalod, I kept thinking of this tiny female. Her beauty, her spirit, and the way she made my skin sing.

"We're a simple people," I said. "We only wish to live. Without young, our species will die."

"You raise them to fight the dresalods."

"None have matured enough yet for battle. But I imagine they'd be as eager to protect our city as their parents. We either fight or we allow the dresalods to overrun us."

"There must be something permanent you can do."

"We haven't discovered it yet."

Her face went pensive. "You chased me in the forest. Grabbed me and brought me here."

"I didn't come to your village to find a mate. The high prince wishes to continue his line and his father treasures his son."

"Ah." She looked pensive. "You were there to guard him."

"And then I heard your voice."

"You were overcome with lust?" She held up her hand. "No, that can't be true. If you were, you would've . . ."

"Fucked you right away?"

Her snort rang out. "You're using my words."

"I imagine everyone in your village believes this to be true. They must see us as beasts like the shaydes."

"We have no reason to think anything else, though no one believes you'd kill us. Why would you when you need us to produce young?" Her fingertips traced across my chest, and my heart thudded once. Twice. Then galloped.

My pendant flickered, but like me, it watched. Waited. Once I claimed her fully, it would no longer glow. Not until I handed it down to my eldest, and it lit up when they found their fated mate.

"Each female claimed in the woods is treasured," I said. "Cherished. How can we do anything else? You're here to give us something we ache for above all else."

"Do my wishes play any role in this?"

"I've told you I won't take you until you beg me to do so. One could consider this as giving into your wishes."

Her chin lifted and her gaze darkened. "I've told you I won't beg you to fuck me."

There was her spunk again. It would be foolish to believe she'd softened to me quickly.

No, when I finally claimed this female, it would be in a fiery rush.

And she'd meet me more than halfway.

CHAPTER 12

RHOSLYN

I scrambled out of his arms and put distance between us.

His cock had started to rise, and my body had responded. Heat rocked through me, centering in my core.

Soon, he'd need to rest. He'd insist I must lie with him.

He was right that he wouldn't need to force me. I'd willingly submit to his claiming.

Even now, his sardonic gaze tracked me like a hunter with prey. Rising, he strode toward the stairs. "Come. Your first task is at hand, tiny mate."

"I'm not fucking you," I squeaked, staring about wildly.

His low laugh rang out. "Not yet, lovely one. But soon. Come." He barked out the command once more. "I need to bathe, and you will assist me. I'm too weary for rutting at the moment."

Alright, I could help him with his bath. My hands shook and my skin prickled in a way I didn't like. I was beginning to crave him, and I didn't like that either. "No fucking after your bath either."

"We shall see." Patience ruled his voice. How long before it snapped?

"You need to know that I'm not a maiden." I started up the stairs behind him.

"Neither am I."

I frowned as we reached the next level. "How old are you?"

"Thirty."

Five years older than me. "Despite your bragging, there are few females here. Do you mean you've been with males?"

He twisted a few levers mounted along the side of the stone tub, sending steaming water gushing into the center, filling it quickly.

"I don't scorn such a thing," he said. "Though it isn't something I'm drawn to."

"You said you've been with others."

"Just one. Not others." His steely gaze met mine. "There was a woman I thought I might someday mate with, though she wasn't my true mate. Ten years ago, she was killed by the shaydes along with my mother."

My breath caught. No wonder he behaved in a harsh,

angry manner. "I'm sorry." He must mourn both of them greatly.

"She was a good female." He removed eight blades of varying sizes from the straps around his waist, placing them in a cabinet I'd missed mounted on the wall. He started untying his loincloth.

My heart stung at the thought he'd cared for another, though I had no right to feel jealous, especially about a poor woman who'd been murdered by the creatures from the sea.

As he stripped, I took note of the shadows of early bruises and the deep gashes on his torso, thighs, and arms. A slash cut from his right eye, across the cheek below it, and ended at his chin. It no longer bled, but it had. The smear told me he'd swiped the wetness away and continued fighting.

"You're wounded." It was all I could do to hold back the urge to fret and flutter around him. I had no herbs, no bandages to heal him.

"This is nothing." His grim gaze slid my way as he tugged the last of the loincloth out from between his legs.

I pivoted sharply, my face heating.

His low chuckle rang out. "You told me you weren't a maiden."

"That doesn't mean I want to see your cock."

"You don't need to see it, only feel it when it's buried deep inside you."

I flushed all over, but the ache in my core told me the sensation didn't come from embarrassment.

I wanted him. Damn me.

"I won't rut with you today, so you can turn around and do your duty without fear." Laughter came through in his voice.

"Somehow, I'm not feeling any easier after that statement." But I did turn, finding him facing away from me, stepping over the side of the tub. His sizeable balls dangled between his legs, and his cock projected well beyond them. It was thick and veiny and had nubs along the sides. How strange and oddly appealing, though I wasn't sure why. Just seeing them made my pulse pick up and my breathing go ragged.

He sunk into the tub and leaned back, spreading his arms wide on the sides. His groan of pleasure rippled across my skin.

My clit throbbed. *All* of me throbbed.

"Come, tiny mate," he said. "Wash my back. My wounds, too. And if you prove your worth with that, I'll permit you to wash my cock."

CHAPTER 13
JAUS

Each time I taunted my tiny mate, I was pulling lightning from the sky. If I didn't take care, it would blast through me. I couldn't seem to resist teasing Rhoslyn, then sitting back and watching her fume.

She didn't want to bathe me, and I well understood why. She felt forced into this relationship, though I somewhat did as well. However, it was my role as her mate to show her she could not only trust me but also take joy in what we could build together.

How had I gone from denying her to aching to possess her? Facing death once more could've played a role.

Was this a betrayal of my vow to myself to never love another like my mother had my father? Some might say yes.

I didn't know, and I was much too tired to analyze it

right now. Each time I faced death could be my last. I needed to focus on this moment and ignore the rest.

She crept up behind me and stood at the side of the tub, breathing fast as she stared down at me. I handed her a small scrap of cloth over my shoulder.

"Back," I said, shifting forward.

With a huff, she dipped the fabric into the water and tentatively started wiping with gentle strokes. Much too soothing. I could maintain my walls much better if she was rough.

"At this rate," I grumbled. "It'll take you all night to wash my back."

The cloth plopped in the water in front of me, splashing my face. "Do it yourself, then."

Lifting it, I wrung it out and held it out to her again. "I don't wish to do this myself. It's your role as my mate to bathe me."

I could almost see the color rising in her face, the irritation blazing in her eyes. I loved it when she snapped and snarled.

"You're covered with cuts," she whispered. "Bruises. I don't want to hurt you."

For a fraction of time, I savored the idea that she felt protective of me, until I remembered her brandishing a knife more than once with the intention of slicing my belly wide open.

"I wish to be clean," I said reasonably. "I'm not worried about pain." In fact, I barely felt any as she pressed harder, creating broad circles with the cloth on my back.

My cock stirred, sensing how close she was.

I wasn't a green male. I could maintain control of my body—or so I told myself.

But as she started running the cloth across my chest and down my arms, taking care to delicately wash each finger, I wasn't sure that I actually could. Her simple touch was dangerously seductive and unlike anything I'd ever felt before. I'd cared for Avella; we grew up together. We were friends, and I was confident that what we had would grow into more. I could see now that we were both incredibly young back then.

She'd never sparked my Azuris pendant, something that bothered her more than me. She was a good female, kind and caring. It was natural we would mate once we matured.

"Tip your head back," Rhoslyn said. Did she realize a subtle tremor came through in her voice or that she kept gliding her tongue across her lips? Her eyes had hooded with a heat I suspected would match my own.

Such was the way with true mates.

She gently washed my hair, taking care not to get soap in my eyes. Her gentle ministrations lulled me, but I'd be unwise to fall asleep. She'd seen where I placed my knives, and I hadn't had enough time yet to convince her she wanted to be with me.

"Do my legs," I said, lifting one and propping the heel on the side of the tub.

She did so willingly, taking care when she encountered gashes and cuts.

Only one place left to wash.

Her gaze kept shooting in that direction, and if she kept at it, my cock would soon be raging.

"I'll wash the rest," I said gruffly.

The cloth dropped from her limp hand, and she backed away from the tub. I made quick work of finishing my body while she moved about, lifting my loincloth and placing it in the washbasin.

"You'll find a drying sheet in that cabinet." I pointed to the one mounted beside the one holding my weapons. "Bring it over and help dry me."

"You can't dry yourself?" she asked with a sneer.

Her softness had faded fast.

"I can, but I won't."

With a grumble, she grabbed a cloth and, spreading it wide, strode toward me as I stepped from the tub and released the plug to allow it to drain.

Her gaze remained on my chest, but that was just as well. If she kept staring at my cock, it would respond to her interest.

She rubbed my body briskly.

"Take care with my wounds, tiny mate," I chided.

Her breath sucked in fast. "I'm sorry."

"You haven't hurt me." Yet. Funny how I was beginning to believe she one day could.

My heart is not getting involved, I shouted to myself.

But no matter how loudly my mind yelled, my heart refused to listen. It tightened whenever she came near.

"Grab a tunic and pants from my wardrobe," I said.

She scurried over to do so and held them out at arm's length, her eyes trained on the wall behind me.

I dressed quickly.

As I finished, her eyes flashed up to meet mine, and I was stunned to find hunger there.

"Have you eaten?"

"I did earlier."

Was the hunger directed toward me? How intriguing.

"Go to the kitchen and prepare me a meal." I nudged my head in that direction.

She flew to the stairs and hurried down them with me following at a more sedate pace. My bones ached. My skin stung in places. And I couldn't wait to lie in my bed.

She'd dozed as I flew Feyla through the night, but I'd remained on high alert. Just because shaydes and dresalods couldn't fly didn't mean there weren't other threats that might attack from the sky.

A warrior would be unwise to let down his guard.

Especially with his tiny human mate.

CHAPTER 14

RHOSLYN

I served Jaus a meal, and he ate with exuberance. After, he leaned back in his chair and gave me a nod. "You're doing well, mate."

Sitting forward, I gave him a smile. "Thank you." Why was I preening from his praise? I didn't need or want him.

My body suggested otherwise. Each groan of appreciation he released as he ate shot through me, centering between my legs, making me throb.

He crinkled his eyes at me where I sat perched on the edge of a chair across from him. "I might just keep you."

My snort shot out. "We'll see about that."

"Come now. You don't love me already?"

If I didn't know better, I'd think longing lurked in his dark eyes. He'd flown all through the night. Battled the moment we arrived here. He was just tired. I didn't see anything else in his gaze.

Hopefully, he was too tired to play a seduction game with my body tonight. I wasn't foolish enough to think he'd somehow make me beg him to take me just by watching me putter about his chamber or make him a decent meal. If I didn't take care, he'd battle through my defenses as easily as he'd defeated the dresalods, then claim victory over my body.

The thought of lying beneath him made my skin prickle.

I swallowed hard, wondering how I'd resist him.

"Tomorrow, we'll go to a place near the market and buy you clothing. Within the next week or so, I must also visit the king. You'll go with me then as well."

That was a surprise. Me, meet the king of the orcs?

Oh, now I knew why he said I'd go with him. "You don't trust me here alone."

"If I felt that way, I wouldn't have left you here even if fifteen legions of dresalods were attacking."

"You would've." I shook my head. "Your sense of duty is too strong to sit here with me while your fellow orcs battle."

"You're right in that." He rose and placed his plate in the sink. "I'll bring you with me because I wish to introduce you to the king."

Interesting.

Passing me, he glided his fingertips across my shoulders. Even through my blouse, I could feel the heat of his touch. My skin flashed with desire.

"Come, tiny mate," he said as he walked out of the

kitchen. "Night has fallen, and you need to bathe before we go to bed. I won't lie beside you when you stink."

I was grateful he threw out the taunt because it made it easier for me to shore up my wall. With a grumble, I followed him, not realizing until we stood in the bathing chamber that I hadn't protested doing what he asked.

Was my will to resist him fading already? It must be. I needed to gird it up, though I wasn't sure how.

"Will you leave me alone to bathe?" I asked as he replaced the plug and turned the levers to fill the tub once more.

The thought of him bathing *me* made my skin flush all over.

"Who will wash your back if I leave the room?"

My laugh burst out because teasing came through in his voice. "I'll find a way to reach."

"I offer my services to you, lovely mate." He bowed low toward me, appearing almost regal in his simple tunic and pants.

"*Seductive* services, you mean."

"Surely you don't expect me to offer you any other?" The curl of his lips made me heat up even more. It was a good thing males couldn't easily tell when a woman was aroused.

"If you're tired, you can go to bed," I said.

"I won't do that until you're ready to join me."

This was going to be the toughest situation I'd faced in my life. "At least turn your back while I undress."

"I'll soon see everything. Why play shy now?"

I'd resist him as long as I could. "Would you mind fetching the bag I brought with me?"

"Of course, tiny mate."

I'd helped pack such bags in the past, and I remembered each held one nightgown, three simple skirts that could be gathered at the waist with a tie to ensure a proper fit, and three loose blouses. No shoes, but there was no way to adjust them to size. And no undergarments. I'd wash out the ones I wore now, and they should be dry by morning. I'd keep the nightgown tucked about my thighs while I slept.

He took the stairs to the lower level.

Maybe he realized I was shy about this and was willing to accommodate my needs. Or maybe he truly was gentle enough that he wanted to give me a bit of space. Whatever his reasoning, I welcomed it, quickly stripping and stepping into the tub, sinking down into the water until it swirled across my chin.

Tipping my head back to rest it on the side of the tub, I moaned at how amazing a hot bath felt. I'd only bathed in the river or run a cold wet cloth over the vital areas within our home when it was too unbearable to think of breaking the ice on the river's surface. The memory of plunging myself into the frigid depths made me shiver even now.

The sound of my bag dropping onto the floor beside me made me sit up fast, my eyes opening.

A tic throbbed in Jaus's brow as he took in my body mostly submerged in the water. His cock tented the front of his pants, and it was all I could do not to reach out and run my fingertip down the fabric-covered length.

This orc was much too tempting. The few times I'd been with the other guy had been so fleeting and dissatisfying, I hadn't asked for more.

I suspected I'd ask for more from Jaus—no, I worried I'd *beg*.

My huff slipped out, and I latched onto bravado to get me through this moment. "Don't you have anything better to do than stare at me?"

"What do you suggest?"

"Wash the gook off your mace."

"I did it before I returned home." He held up his big hands. "And I washed my hands in the bath not long after." He lifted my soiled clothing and carefully placed it in the sink, running water over it along with his loincloth.

I'd discovered who kept his quarters neat and tidy.

Was he lonely here all by himself?

I didn't like that I felt sympathy for him. I needed to keep up my walls. Otherwise, he'd claim my heart along with my body.

"You could go rest somewhere," I said. "Let me bathe in peace."

"But you look so lovely in my tub, tiny mate. Why would I wish to be anywhere else?" He took one step toward me. "I could wash your back."

"I told you I'd take care of that myself."

He came another step closer. "I'd be happy to massage your feet."

"They're ticklish. I'll wiggle all around the tub while you did it, splashing water on the floor."

Stepping closer, he shrugged. "Maybe I like getting things wet."

He meant me. I could feel my body responding to his nearness. In my past relationship, I'd let the other male do what he'd pleased, but it had felt so dry.

I suspected I'd be anything but dry if Jaus touched me.

"Are you sure you don't want me to . . . wash you anywhere?" He stood right beside the tub, staring down, though I appreciated that he kept his attention on my face.

Maybe if I let him do this, do whatever he wanted in this moment, he'd stop taunting me. He kept daring me to give him everything, and I hated to think I was tempted. Once I gave in, I suspected he'd leave me alone except for some random fucking. I could stare at the ceiling like I had in the past and think about herbs while he did it.

"Tell you what," I said, lifting the cloth from the water, "wash whatever you please. I believe it's almost time for us to go to bed."

CHAPTER 15
JAUS

She'd called my dare. Or had it truly been a dare? I wanted her more than I liked, but she was my true mate, chosen for me by my clan pendant and the very fates above. I wasn't a male who believed much in the spiritual side of life, but there was no denying its glow and the mirrored heat flaring inside me right now.

Stooping down, I took the cloth from her limp hand. She watched me intently with true desire blazing in her eyes.

I'd been looking forward to my first attempt at seduction.

"I'm not going to rut with you, mate," I said, my voice coming out in a growl. Somehow, she'd turned this on me, taking over the dominant position while I gave in to whatever might make her happy.

"Not yet, you said," she chided with a subtle smile.

She was trying to tease me even in this. "Not *tonight*." Everything was fair game tomorrow.

"Are you too tired?"

My cock wasn't.

My body? Somewhat.

My soul? I didn't want to think about my soul right now.

"Lean forward," I grumbled.

She did so, and I began rubbing the cloth across her skin, gliding it all the way down her spine and across the top of her lush ass.

Focus on this task, I told myself. Not how soft her skin felt beneath my fingertips, nor how her eyes had closed, showing she was savoring the relaxing sensation.

I moved to her arms, taking infinite care with her fragile skin. She was so much smaller and delicate than me, though lush and curvaceous, just the way I liked a female. It was too easy to picture myself gripping her ass tight while I pumped my cock deep within her from behind.

Her soft moan slipped out.

My cock throbbed where it smacked against my abs.

I slid the cloth over her breasts, gulping when her nipples hardened. What I would give to suck first one, then the other, into my mouth. I'd cup them gently and stare into her eyes while I gave her pleasure.

Working the fabric lower, I nearly came when she leaned back and spread her legs apart, inviting me to take this in any direction I craved.

I craved *her*.

Only her.

I sensed I would for a lifetime.

She was going to be the death of me, and I'd willingly succumb in her arms.

Her gasp rang out when I stroked the cloth over her clit and down across her opening. Her hips lifted as I continued to rub, making sure I teased her clit just enough to tempt her but never quite giving it full attention.

When I moved the cloth aside and slid a fingertip inside her, her eyelids snapped open. Her sultry gaze fixed on mine, and her lips parted in a sigh.

Leaning closer, I captured her mouth, delving deeply with my tongue. She didn't fight me. No, she clutched my shoulders and moaned, her tongue teasing across mine.

I kept my fingers between her legs. As I kissed her, groans erupted up my throat. I found her clit with my thumb and continued to move my finger deep within her. Even after the slosh of the water, she was still wet from her inner juices.

She accepted my finger so well that I added another, slowly pumping them inside her while my tongue mimicked the action in her mouth.

Her nails bit into my shoulders, and if I tried to break free, I had no doubt she'd claw me.

No need to worry about that. I was here for as long as she needed me.

A flick of my hand released the plug, and the water

gushed down through the pipes, exposing all of her to my view and touch.

While I continued to fuck her with my fingers and stroke her clit, I kissed along her jawline. She tipped her head back and gasped, her hands moving up to my horns, grabbing onto them like I ached to have her grab onto my cock.

I sucked her nipple into my mouth and moved my fingers faster.

She whimpered and bucked against me, driving my fingers deeper, and it was all I could do not to rip away my pants, lift her, and push her down hard on my cock.

Soon. For now, I only wanted to show her pleasure.

Her cries echoed around us, and her hips moved frantically, pushing up to meet my hand with each thrust. I pressed harder on her clit with my thumb while flicking my tongue across first one and then the other nipple.

She came all at once with a soft moan, her body convulsing around my fingers.

I kept moving them until her shudders ceased and the pump of her hips slowed.

Pulling out my fingers, I sucked on them one at a time.

She watched me, and I knew right then that I was going to lose my heart to this tiny female.

CHAPTER 16

RHOSLYN

I'd never experienced anything like what he'd done with his fingers. I wanted him to do it again.

Should I tell him?

No, that would set me up to be mocked. He'd savor knowing he could make me crave him so quickly.

Damn, I wasn't a woman who liked to beg.

If I wasn't careful, he'd capture my heart and mock me for giving it to him so easily.

He grabbed a drying cloth from the cabinet and lifted me out of the tub, placing my feet gently on the floor, then proceeded to rub me all over until I was dry.

By the time he'd finished, I could barely remain on my feet. My knees shook from desire, and I was much too close to demanding he put his fingers inside me again. The words hovered on the tip of my tongue.

"I need my nightgown," I said, pointing to the bag still lying on the floor.

"You'll wear no clothing while you lie in my bed, tiny mate."

Before I could voice a protest, he swept me up and carried me into the bedroom, laying me on the soft surface.

His covetous gaze glided slowly down my body like a caress. He wanted me. There was no denying that. But could wanting turn into something more?

Sitting, I yanked the covers up over my body, hiding it from his view.

I should close my eyes and pretend to fall asleep fast. Instead, I watched as he stripped, and this time, I didn't look away when he exposed his cock.

Big. Already figured that one out.

Thick. Ditto.

The nubs along the sides I'd seen in his quick flash quivered, and I could only imagine how they would feel if he was buried inside me. Would it hurt at first like it had with the other guy? The pain was fleeting, but after that, each episode had gone so quickly, I hadn't had time to decide if I'd liked it or not.

I was beginning to believe I'd like it a lot if Jaus was the one pumping inside me. And that presented a dilemma. What if I fell for him and he didn't feel the same?

I wanted to yank on my hair and howl—much like I had while he moved his fingers inside me. This time, though, my howl would contain frustration. Wanting him, let alone begging him to claim me, could leave me floundering.

My goal should be returning to my sister, not remaining here to be Jaus's plaything.

Of course, my sister would soon marry, and then I'd be alone.

Realizing that this meant I could stay here, and she'd be safe with her new husband, only made my irritation gouge deeper inside me.

I didn't like how he was scrambling my life or how he made me need something I couldn't define.

Lifting the blankets, he climbed in beside me as naked as me, tugging the blankets up to his waist.

He turned me until my back faced him and tucked his full length tight against my spine.

"Sleep, tiny mate," he said softly.

His stiff cock probed between us, but I wasn't going to beg. I'd hold off doing that until I was sure that he was falling for me just like I was for him.

Shit.

That thought did not occur to me!

I wouldn't love him.

With that in mind, I drifted to sleep surrounded by his arms and his warmth.

I was startled awake to sunbeams poking through the windows above and a subtle sound that for some reason made me think dresalods were scrambling their way up the building.

What if one got inside?

I leaped from the bed and started to rush around it but slammed into something hard and solid. Yelping, I fled backward, tripping over something else and falling on my ass. My breasts bounced and my legs splayed wide.

I caught Jaus's sardonic gaze traveling from my breasts to the juncture between my thighs. "Are you alright?"

"Yes." Only my pride was hurt. And my butt.

"We need to eat breakfast," he said in a husky voice. "But there's still time left, tiny mate."

"For what?" My mouth had gone dry, and there was no way I'd ever be able to swallow again.

Lifting me, he laid me on the bed. He loomed over me before moving downward, kissing my belly as he passed. He spread my thighs wide and grinned up at me. "For me to eat *you*, of course."

Why was I laying limply beneath him? I should flee. Find a place to hide until his lust had faded.

Sadly, he wasn't the only one who lusted. I'd spent most of the night reliving what happened in the tub, dreaming of him doing it again.

Eat me, huh? I wasn't completely sure what he meant, but after what he'd done with his fingers last night, I couldn't make myself scramble out from beneath him to flee.

He'd turned me into a needy thing, a female who craved his touch, and I didn't like it one bit.

But when he pushed his mouth against me and sucked on the sensitive bud he'd stroked last night, I barked out a gasp.

I clutched his horns as he continued to suck me, his tongue flicking and stroking until I lost all control and shrieked, bucking up and biting my tongue to keep from begging.

His finger took over from his mouth on my sensitive coil of nerves, and his tongue moved downward to slide into my passage. His fingers joined his tongue, alternating with what felt like three or more fingers pushing inside me, his long tongue flicking against my inner walls at the same time.

I was a solid mass of need, a lump of clay eager for him to mold, and there was no denying he was too good at seduction.

When his fingers moved faster, and his tongue found the hard bud at the top once more, my eyes rolled back in my head, and I lost all control. Moaning, I yanked on his horns. I thrust my hips up to meet his fingers. I spread my legs wider.

I rode his hand while it rode me until my body crashed, giving into the same pleasure he'd given me last night.

When I'd finally stopped shuddering with pleasure, he looked up at me with a sultry smile. It was all I could do not to grin right back at him.

"Get up, tiny mate." He backed off and stood at the end of the bed, his possessive gaze locked on my wide-spread form. "You need to make me breakfast."

CHAPTER 17
JAUS

Rhoslyn consumed my every thought, and I didn't like it. With Avella, I'd been able to separate my feelings for her from the work I needed to do. When I wasn't with her, I barely thought about her.

Yesterday, it was all I could do to focus on fighting off the dresalods. I'd become distracted too many times, fretting about Rhoslyn until I was yanked back into the situation with a dresalod about to kill me.

I rarely suffered wounds in battle, and the gouges and cuts I'd received yesterday from their claws were payment for being distracted. They still stung and would serve as a reminder that I needed to separate whatever feelings I might have for my mate from the rest of my life.

This wasn't an easy thing to do as I went down two flights of stairs to the kitchen with her following. She'd quickly tugged on a skirt and blouse that were much too large for her.

"I need to buy you clothing immediately," I snapped, hating to see her appearing this rumpled.

"We're back there again, are we?" she asked, taking bread and preserves from the cool box and placing them on the table.

"Back where? What do you speak of?"

"You acting grumpy while I try to remain cheerful." A scowl transformed her face, making her even more appealing when it shouldn't. "I'm telling you right now, I'm not playing sunshine to your snarly orc demeanor. You'll soon find out I can be as snarly as you."

"I am not grumpy or snarly." But even I could hear the growl in my voice.

Her smile flashed so briefly I almost missed it. "Do you have butter? I don't see any around."

"Why would I need butter?" This time, I kept my voice neutral. I was not grumpy. I was an even-tempered orc. Everyone said so.

"Because it tastes good." Her lips twisted, and her eyes gleamed with irritation.

If I kissed her, I bet that expression would disappear. I could replace it with that limpid look I was beginning to crave. And moans of pleasure.

But the thought of doing that to her made me cringe inside. I didn't want to manipulate her with sex. Yes, I'd taunted her with the notion of begging me to sink my cock into her, but I needed her to want what we did as much as me. That was the basis of my claim.

And that irritated me too. She was my mate, the female who'd carry my orclings. Why was I thinking of her as anything else?

My snarl ripped out of me.

Her eyebrows lifted. "You can't even maintain a cinnamon roll hero for ten seconds."

"What is this cinnamon roll hero?"

"Not you, that's for sure." She lowered plates onto the table and sliced the bread, putting three slices on one plate and one on another. Sitting, she waved to the plate with three. "Eat."

"Cinnamon is a spice. It's used in a roll." I lifted the bread. "A roll crafted something like this. And I'm already a hero." I flashed my tusks her way.

She rolled her eyes. "I'll give you that. You behaved in a heroic manner yesterday."

My spine stiffened. "I behave in a heroic manner all the time."

"Maybe it's a work thing. You're dedicated, and it shows."

I liked it when she spoke well of me.

Actually, I didn't need her to like me. I grumbled as I spread preserves on the bread and took a big bite, speaking around it. "We'll go into town and—"

"You can leave me here. I promise I . . ."

I lifted one brow her way, watching her squirm. "You can promise you won't run or leave me, pretty mate?"

"I don't feel a pressing need to flee at the moment."

"You enjoy my touch," I said smugly.

Her lips thinned. "What makes you think that?"

"The way you moaned. The shriek that burst from your lips when you came." It echoed in my mind, making me ache to take her back to my bed and show her all over again that she couldn't resist me. No, I'd sweep everything off the table and take her on the surface. "You shouldn't feel embarrassed by how you respond to my attention. You're behaving as a good mate should."

"I'm not good." She gripped her knife tight. Would she actually attempt to stab me with it? If she did, *then* I would lay her on the table and distract her. It would only be fair. "Truly," she said. "You might soon discover I'm *very* bad."

"Bad works just as well as good for me." I gave her a sunny smile, pleased with my mate despite her possibly vicious tendencies. She'd bear me orclings with the same fire, and who could complain about something like that?

"You mentioned taking me to the king soon," she said. "Why would he want to meet me?"

"Why wouldn't he?"

"Because I'm . . . I'm not really sure what my role here is."

"You're my mate. It's an illustrious position."

Why did she roll her eyes at my statement?

"Back in my village," she said. "I went to the woods each day to collect herbs I used to treat ailments. I'm used to spending my time in that way, not meeting royalty or shopping."

"You're a healer."

"I am." She delicately took a bite of her bread, chewing carefully and with her mouth closed.

Realizing crumbs were raining down the front of my tunic and that I was gnawing through my second slice of bread in big gulps, I slowed my pace and ate with more care. The teachings of my upbringing echoed in my mind.

"I learned everything I know about healing from my mother," she said. Pain flickered in her eyes, and I barely suppressed the urge to gather her in my arms and hold her forever. "My parents died ten years ago. Shaydes attacked them while they were traveling to another village. They shouldn't have left their shelter that night, but they were rushing to get back to me and my sister. We were staying with friends. I . . ."

She squeezed her eyes shut, opening them again and displaying so much devastation, it kicked me in the gut. I lowered my bread onto my plate. "I raised my sister after that. My mother was a well-respected healer, and she taught me how to find the right herbs in the forest and how to prepare them."

"I'm sorry. I, too, have lost family. My mother was killed ten years ago during a shayde attack that deci-mated my people."

"With your mate?" She traced her finger along the edge of her plate, not looking my way.

"We hadn't mated yet."

Her nod jerked out. "So much unfulfilled promise."

"We . . . I cared for her, but I realize now that it was more as a friend, not a lover."

"Oh." She lifted her bread then put it back down on her plate. "You're the only one left of your family?"

"My father still lives, but we don't have a good relationship."

"I'm sorry. Surely, he's proud of you. You hold a highly respected position in the kingdom."

Not wanting to discuss my father, I shrugged off her comment. "I've worked hard to show the fates they were correct in allowing me to survive not just the shayde but many dresalod attacks."

"Battling all the time is such a burden, isn't it?"

I'd never thought of it in that way. "It is my duty. How can I do anything else?"

"Some might've curled up inside and hidden rather than challenging themselves to always try harder."

I scoffed. "You didn't do this."

She looked up, blinking. "You're right. I was eighteen when the shaydes killed my parents, and Lyneth was only thirteen."

"The shaydes have caused a lot of pain for both of us. Is Lyneth back at the village?"

Picking up her bread, she stared at it for a long while. "She is. She's going to marry her childhood sweetheart soon. They've been inseparable since they were little."

"It was the same for me and Avella." My mood

turned pensive. "For most of my life, everyone expected us to mate."

"You're fortunate you had her in your life."

"She was a good friend." That was just it. She hadn't sparked my fire like Rhoslyn did. "As I said, she didn't spark my Azuris pendant." I tapped it where it hung, as always, on a leather band around my neck. "But I did care for her."

"It's hard to lose those we love."

Had I loved Avella? Of course, but . . . I didn't want to think about how my feelings for Rhoslyn were different, fierier and more vibrant. More lasting. That was unfair to the female who'd cared for me, who'd looked forward to our mating.

We finished our meal and cleaned the dishes and Rhoslyn looked up at me with a strange expression on her face when I dried and put away the items she washed in the sink.

"Are you ready to leave?" I asked after I'd put the last item away. "We'll return before the midday meal. I have work to do after that."

"Let me run upstairs for just a moment. I'll be right back." She didn't take long, returning with the cloth bag she'd carried with her yesterday, though it was now empty. She shot me a nervous smile. "Ready."

I grabbed my mace and tucked the shaft into the sheath on my back.

Her soft smile fell. "Do you expect the dresalods to attack again?"

"We chased them away yesterday. If they're wise, they'll hide deep beneath the surface forever." They were most likely regrouping, waiting for more of their spawn to grow large enough to join the legion before they attacked again.

She followed me to the hatch on the lowest level of my home that took up only the top section of the tower. "I didn't see this area."

"Would you have tried to escape this way if you had?" I was only teasing, and when her eyes lit up, I could tell she knew.

"Maybe." Her lips quivered. She was so pretty when she struggled not to smile.

Yesterday, I would've snarled at the thought of her fleeing from me. Today . . . It didn't seem to bother me.

Perhaps I had a bit of the sweet roll she desired inside me after all.

The stairs exited out between this building and the next, and I took her hand, leading her onto the street. I told myself I held onto her to ensure we weren't separated, but foot traffic was light.

Prizing honesty above all else, I'd never been one to lie to myself.

I liked holding her hand.

"It's the mate bond," I said.

"What is?" Her gaze shot to my pendant. "It's not glowing."

"Because I gave you pleasure."

"I've never believed in magic."

I shrugged. "Me either, but clan pendants always know."

"Where do they come from?"

"Each family in the clan has them. They're passed down from the parents to the eldest, be that a son or a daughter. The elders always say they provide guidance."

"Not the best guidance if your pendant lit up for me."

I pulled her to a stop before we joined the main thoroughfare. "Why would you say that?"

"You don't like me."

I lowered my voice. "I very much enjoyed your response to my tongue."

Her face pinkened, and I stood there stunned for a moment, watching the varying hues on her face. Why was I so fascinated by this human creature?

"That was a physical thing," she said with a sigh. "That has nothing to do with liking."

I gave myself time to think before responding, partly because I didn't know exactly what to say to her. How much did I dare reveal?

I wasn't exactly sure what I wanted to do with my lovely mate. When I left with Madr for the Hunt, I anticipated returning to the city and resuming my regular duties, not catering to the needs of a woman. Now I found myself aching to see her smile, to *please her*, and not only sexually.

The light went out in her eyes. "You don't need to say anything. I understand. You were forced into this as much as me."

"It takes time for affection to grow." I felt like that didn't quite express the feelings growing inside me, but I wasn't sure how to name them. "We only recently met."

"You don't need to love your mate, you mean," she said bitterly. "You don't even need to like her—*me*. It's clear that even disliking me, you'll find a way to plant your orclings inside me."

"I ask you to give this time." And to give me time to determine what was going on inside my heart. "History shows that those fated for each other share the strongest love. Does it suddenly bloom within the heart, or does it grow slowly? I don't know the answer to that."

She huffed. "I doubt I'm going to love you no matter how long we're together."

What if I wanted her to love me?

Grumbling and feeling much too uncertain about all this, I urged her to walk once more, keeping a tight hold on her hand as we joined the many orcs using this main course to take them to the center of the city.

"Where does the king live?" she asked, peering around.

"The king's main castle was built on one of the taller hills on the mountain side of the city. The family owns smaller palaces, of course, and he often spends the hot months in the one near the sea."

"We'll walk when we visit him tomorrow?"

"I wouldn't bother Feyla for something like that."

As we traveled into the center of the city, she gaped

at everything. I tried to see it as she did, as someone who was new to the kingdom.

I suppose if I had recently arrived in the city, I'd react in the same way. The streets were lined with magnificent silver buildings that rose two and three stories high. They must appear majestic to her after living in a small village behind a stone wall.

Grand towers stood on the top of the buildings, their peaks proudly flying vibrant flags that fluttered in the wind.

It was the perfect day to walk, and our footsteps were light on the cobblestone street. I was proud to show my city off to her—and to show *her* off to those around us.

Some orcs came to a stop when they saw her, their jaws unhinging, while others just stared, their dark eyes wide. Women were not that unusual here; after all, we'd collected mates during the Hunt for ten years now. Prior to that, a few women encountered orcs, and the couples fell in love. They'd also moved here since women were accepted in our city while orcs were not welcome in theirs.

I was proud of my people, and if humans couldn't see that our value sunk deep beneath our greenish-golden skin, then they weren't worth our time.

"Such unique architecture," she whispered, gaping around. "Everything's so big. It makes me feel the size of a child."

"You're tiny." *My* tiny mate.

We nearly ran into two orcs from a different clan

who'd gone with the group the other night but hadn't been chosen to hunt.

They both grinned, their gazes only for Rhoslyn.

"Your hunt found success," one said, his brow furrowing as his eyes met mine. "You're incredibly fortunate as always, Jaus."

"Too fortunate, I'd say." The second fingered his weapon.

Rhoslyn's attention flicked between us, and she stepped closer to me.

Noting them staring at her longer than I liked, I reached back to finger the hilt of my mace. A snarl ripped up my throat, and Rhoslyn swallowed deeply.

Their eyes narrowed, but they said nothing, continuing along the street.

Turning, I watched until they'd mixed in with the crowd.

"I'm sorry," Rhoslyn said so softly, I barely heard her above those hawking their wares in the marketplace ahead.

"It's not your fault."

She grunted, and we continued walking. I kept her close to my side and glared at anyone who so much as looked her way.

Stopping partway down the street, I gestured to a shop on a corner between a side street and the main thoroughfare. "We can buy butter here."

Her face darkened with color. Why this time? "That's sweet of you."

"I like butter too."

"Oh." Her shoulders drooped.

"What else do you like to eat?" I asked as we went inside.

"Anything, really."

"Tell me."

She shrugged. "Fruit. Vegetables. The bread we had this morning was good."

I collected things in a basket as she spoke, and when she lifted a bottle of honey but put it back quickly, I added that to my basket as well.

"I want a lot of butter," I told the clerk.

"This much?" he asked, holding up a tub the size of his head.

"Yes."

When I noted her looking toward barrels of hard candy, I added those to my order. The same with the dried fish she admired. And the dried meat. The odd vegetables her glance took in joined the rest.

"Anything else, Commander?" the clerk asked.

"Anything else?" I asked Rhoslyn.

She flashed me a sweet smile that made me want to buy everything in the store to keep that look on her face. "Oh, I don't need anything."

"This will be it for now," I said.

The clerk tallied my bill and after I'd paid, put everything in a cloth pouch I tossed over my shoulder.

"You're hungry," she said as we left. "I should've given you more slices of bread this morning."

I *was* hungry but more for her than food. Pondering that notion, I led her down a few more streets, arriving at our next destination. By then, I hadn't decided on anything, and I suspected I wouldn't even if I dwelled on it for the next thirty days.

"We'll get you clothing here," I said gruffly, gesturing to the store.

Her head tilted as she studied the sign, and the most beautiful smile flitted across her face. "There's a woman's head on the sign, not just an orc's."

"Because this shop is owned by Eleri, a human female mated to Odik."

Her breath caught. "Eleri's here in the city?"

"As I said, she's mated to Odik. She works in the city, though she and Odik live with the rest of his clan."

"I remember her vaguely. She joined the Hunt five years ago, though in a more unconventional way. She was a few years older than me, and we weren't close. I can't wait to see her again, though." With a grin shot my way that made my lungs freeze, she pushed open the front door and stepped inside, holding the panel open for me. "Come on. Don't just stand there on the street."

I found a way to breathe and followed her inside.

Someone shrieked in the back of the shop.

Dropping the bag of food, I yanked my mace from its sheathe and thrust Rhoslyn behind me.

I'd kill anyone who threatened my mate.

CHAPTER 18
RHOSLYN

Jaus bristled and hefted his mace.

I peered around him, wondering what was happening, but I only found Eleri weaving slowly around racks of clothing. After suffering a grave injury when she was a child that left her with a bad limp, her parents—living in one of the other villages far from mine—had abandoned her in the woods. If a widower hunter hadn't found and raised her, who knows what might've happened to her? She was only three at the time.

Five years ago, she was accused of murdering the hunter, but I'd never believed her capable of such a horrifying deed. There wasn't anyone kinder or more generous than Eleri. She'd fled the night of the hunt, and no one had heard from her again—though that was the norm for those taken by orcs.

She hobbled over to me, her face filled with reservation.

I braced her shoulders. "Before you say a thing, I want to tell you I never thought you did it."

The reservation didn't leave her face.

"And my suspicion was confirmed when Brigid lay on her deathbed and confessed," I added.

"I saw her leaving our home. I knew she'd done it, but . . ." Eleri's gaze dropped from mine. "I didn't think anyone would believe me."

Most hadn't, though a few of us spoke up for her. The consensus was she'd done it. Why else would she flee?

"You could return to the village if you wanted," I said.

"I don't want to." Eleri's chin lifted. "I'm happy here with Odik. There's no place I'd rather be."

I placed my hand on Jaus's arm to tug him forward to join us.

Looking a bit embarrassed, though I wasn't sure why, he grunted and returned his mace to its sheath.

Did he think Eleri was attacking me?

I wasn't sure what I thought about this grumbly, grouchy orc who seemed determined to thrust himself between me and any threat, let alone a guy who appeared to calm at my touch. For someone who stated he didn't like me, it was a surprise to see him behave in this manner.

Although, he hadn't said he *didn't* like me. He'd been evasive, stating emotions took time. I understood that. Although, in my case, it wasn't taking much time for me to long for him. And no, it wasn't just sexual. The longing had begun before he licked me.

I worried I was succumbing like all the other women caught in the hunt, that I was falling in love with my new husband despite my determination to hold myself back.

"Rhoslyn, when did you arrive in the city?" Eleri exclaimed, holding my forearms and looking me up and down. A true smile filled her face now. She must be relieved to hear everyone knew she hadn't killed Zur. "Actually, I should know the answer to that already. A few days ago, since the Hunt was just held." She studied Jaus, fingering her deep red hair she'd pulled up in the back but left a few tendrils dangling near her face. Her brown eyes sparkled with excitement. "You've mated with the commander, I see."

I wasn't sure we were mated yet, but he'd called me his fated one. He'd said those chosen by clan pendants often fell in love.

I didn't want his love, did I? Maybe . . .

Argh. I didn't want to think about that at all. I'd take the pleasure he offered and call it good enough.

Her hands dropped to her big belly, and from the sharp look in the eyes of the brawny orc who'd followed her to the front of the store, I suspected she'd soon deliver his orcling.

Odik nodded to Jaus. Eleri's mate was the same height and build as Jaus, though his eyes were a startling gold, not the dark brownish-gold I found so appealing in Jaus. He also bristled with weapons, and his pendant was different than Jaus's, a circular disc made up of swirls that must represent air. In his case, a thick stick tightly gripped in his hand, plus a long blade strapped to a sheath on his back.

"This is my mate, Odik." Eleri leaned back against his chest and grinned up at him. "You're going to love it here, as much as you'll love Jaus."

I was determined not to do that, but I didn't say a word. Jaus watched me intently, though I couldn't tell what he was thinking.

"Thus far, it's been quite an interesting experience," I said, a neutral answer.

Eleri's smile fell. "Did you arrive while the dresalods were attacking?"

I nodded. "They're terrifying."

"Our males will protect us with their lives." She stroked Odik's hand resting on her belly.

"When is your orcling due?" I asked.

"Soon." Her smile bloomed again. "This will be our second. We have one son, Zur, named for the man who was like a father to me, and we both hope for a girl child this time, though we'll be happy with another boy."

"Congratulations." Seeing her happy eased my concern somewhat. I still had to reconcile what I might have in the future with Jaus besides amazing bed action. But if the city welcomed me like it appeared they had Eleri, it would be a nice start. I'd miss my sister, but knowing she would be with her love would make it easier for me to build a new life here. At least I no longer needed to worry about Eamon trying to bed me.

Eleri studied my clothing, and I recalled she'd done exquisite embroidery when she lived in the village. "I see you're wearing the latest hunt-wear."

My laugh snorted out. "You're insulting my seamstress skills."

Her smile widened. "If I remember correctly, you trained with your mother and were already a rather skilled healer yourself. I don't believe I remember you sewing much, however."

"You've caught me." I chuckled.

"I need a complete wardrobe for my mate," Jaus said, his arm going around my back as if he was pleased to be standing by my side. "Everyone speaks highly of your skills with clothing."

His gesture pleased me until I realized he was probably pretending so Eleri wouldn't worry. She was happy with Odik, and she'd be sad to think me and Jaus weren't getting along as well.

He'd asked for time, and he was right to make the request. Caring for another didn't happen overnight, no matter how much a male excited me between the blankets.

As I looked up at him, I noted how intently he watched me. There were no threats here for him to vanquish. Perhaps he was gazing at me with the beginnings of caring. He could be happy he was with me.

I'd cling to that for now.

"Let me see what I have." Eleri scanned my front. "I believe I have a few items in your size. I cater to both orcs and humans, though there aren't as many of us here, obviously." Taking my hand, she wove through the shop full of mostly male clothing appropriate for an orc, leading me to a long rack in the back holding gowns, skirts, and adorable blouses. "I have nightgowns and underthings available as well."

"We won't need those," Jaus growled.

Eleri hid her smile behind her hand, winking at me. She leaned close, lowering her voice for my ears alone. "Is he always this grouchy?"

"So far."

"You'll sweeten him up. He's a nice enough male. I've met up with him in the past, and he was always pleasant."

I was waiting for *pleasant* to enter our home, though I had my doubts it would ever happen. Although, he already made more effort to please me than he had when we first met.

He bought butter when he said he didn't need it. I hadn't missed him adding honey to his order after I'd lifted the container and reluctantly placed it back.

There may be hope for us yet.

Eleri's voice dropped even lower. "If it helps, know that Odik and I are as happy today as we were not long after we first met during the hunt. It will be that way for you too."

"How can you know this?" I peered over my shoulder,

finding Jaus and Odik standing close to the front of the shop, staring out the window, talking quietly.

"His pendant flared for you, didn't it?"

I nodded.

She nudged my side. "Then the sex will be amazing, and he'll soon be doing all he can to please you. Before you know it, you'll have an orcling on the way."

"I'm not sure I want children. After raising my sister, I thought my time had passed me by."

She frowned and lifted a skirt off the rack, holding it up against me before clicking her tongue and putting it back. "How old are you?"

"Twenty-five."

"Very young."

"I don't feel young."

"Young enough to please Jaus." She flicked her eyes that way. "He watches you all the time, even now when he speaks with Odik."

A glance over my shoulder confirmed her statement. For whatever reason, my face heated. "I doubt I please him. He's probably worried I'll try to flee, that he must watch me to keep it from happening."

She lifted one eyebrow and pursed her lips. "Will you?"

"If you'd asked me that when I arrived, yes. Now . . ."

"Ah, I well understand." Her arm went around my waist, and she gave me a quick hug. "You've slept in his bed. Even now, his orcling may grow within you."

"We didn't do . . . that." My cheeks got even hotter. I

wasn't used to discussing something like this with another person.

Her face creased before smoothing. "He must be giving you time to adjust like my Odik did."

"You two didn't . . . do that right away?"

"I suspect I would've been willing if he'd pushed for it, but he's a sweet orc. He said he didn't want to claim me until I was ready."

I wasn't going to ask how long that took.

"I was ready rather quickly." A twinkle bloomed in her eyes. "As in all matings, I imagine you'll also be ready rather quickly as well."

I refuse to beg—so far—but how long would it take before he was impossible to resist?

CHAPTER 19

JAUS

Striding along the cobblestone streets toward our home with my mate tucked against my side, I snapped my tusks at any orc who came within an arm's length of her.

"Thank you for my new clothing," she said, looking up at me with an expression I couldn't discern. Thanks, most likely.

Not the affection I hoped . . . I bit back my growl. I didn't want her to love me, did I?

"You're welcome," I said gruffly, shifting our sack of food on my shoulder. "We'll go back when she has more clothing in stock."

"You bought me five outfits already!"

"You deserve three times that many."

Shaking her head, a smile flitted across her lips. "I can only wear one per day. I'll wash what's soiled in between. Realistically, two will do fine."

Two? I scoffed. "That's not enough clothing for *my* mate. And I've thought of hiring someone to do the wash for you." Now, where had that thought come from?

She stopped and orcs streamed around us, studiously avoiding looking at her when they caught my stern eye. "Why would you do that? I can wash and keep our home clean. Prepare our meals as well."

"*Our* home? *Our* meals?"

Her shoulders curled forward. "*Your* home, that is."

I tugged her close and just held her. "It's your home. Your food. My possessions are yours. Always consider it thus." I couldn't resist kissing the top of her head.

The tension fled her body, and I beamed so brightly inside, I was surprised my pendant didn't reflect the feeling.

"Take care, *mate*," she said wryly when we started walking again. "Or I'll begin to suspect you have some cinnamon roll inside you."

Perhaps I did—when it came to her.

As we left the main marketplace, she peered around, oblivious to the attention she drew. "Your city is amazing. So many beautiful buildings. So many beautiful people."

She found orcs attractive, did she? It shouldn't matter to me, but I couldn't stop my heart from expanding three times its normal size. It was getting squished against my ribcage.

"I told you many orcs live here." I struggled to sound

neutral. "That we built our homes from steel for protection from the dresalods."

When had I started softening toward my pretty mate?

From the moment I met her.

"Eleri told me there are six orc clans altogether," she said, seemingly oblivious to my undying attention. "Do they all live in the city?"

"Mostly just the Azuris Clan," I fingered my pendant, "and some of the Lumen Clan, though most of those living within the city walls are part of the royal family."

"Where do the other clans live?"

"One chose to live in the forest, another in an intricate cave system deep within the mountain range. All travel to the city by vox."

As if to punctuate my words, a flight of mounted vox soared overhead. The large group split, some flying toward the sea, others landing on various buildings including the seaside palace.

Had my father arrived? I didn't recognize his vox among the others, but the sunlight glinted off the scales of a few resting on the balcony built into the side of the palace tower. His vox was ruby red, and I spied that color among those on the balcony.

"Eleri has a clothing shop in town. Is Odik part of your clan?"

"He's the caedos or leader of the Zephyr Clan."

"Where do *they* live?" She looked up at me sweetly, almost with what I took for appreciation in her eyes.

My chest puffing, I guided her along the street toward our home. "Odik's clan built homes on tall islands far out in the sea."

She gasped. "The dresalods must threaten them too."

"Sometimes. They're quite good at fighting them off, and their homes are built at the highest points of the island."

She clutched my forearm. "How many orcs die in each battle?"

"Not many. We've learned their weaknesses and enhanced our own skills with the weapons that kill them the easiest. I fight from Feyla's back, for example, and she's quite adept at evading their claws."

"Yet they keep coming, you said."

"They breed and mature fast." And they were eager to eat us.

"You need a permanent solution," she said.

"Short of moving away from the city where we'll then face the shaydes, we have no choice but to remain here."

A frown knit her brow. "Then we need to think of a way to keep them from returning without losing any more orcs."

"They live deep beneath the sea where we can't reach them."

"You've built a wall around the city. Could you build a wall farther out to sea or use . . . a net of some sort to hold them back?"

"These are solid ideas we've considered already. The

dresalods can scale most walls. They find our metal structures more of a challenge."

"How did you craft the metal you use for your buildings?"

Pausing, I tapped a smooth, silver wall gleaming in the sunlight. "We construct the building from wood and attach the metal to the outer surface, using a system that ensures there's almost no seam for them to latch onto."

"The buildings in your city are stunning. As we flew close with Feyla, the city looked like a giant basket full of precious silver jewelry."

"Our system wouldn't work with a wall built up from the sea floor. It would rust and the wood would rot too quickly."

"A net then?"

"They could climb over the top or slice through it with their claws."

She sighed. "I wish I could think of something that would help."

She was new to the city, and her perspective would be different. Maybe she could come up with an idea we hadn't thought of.

"If anyone could think of a way, it would be the king's advisors, and sadly, they've yet to find a solution." I led her down a street exiting the main route.

She nodded pertly. "I'll think about it and let you know if I come up with something."

"Why? I understand not wanting to see others

harmed, but as far as I can see, you don't consider this your home." Would she ever feel she belonged here?

"I'm warming up to the idea." With that, she continued walking.

I scurried—no, I *strode*—to catch up with her and took her hand, squeezing it. It warmed me through when she said things like that.

Talking with her like this, instead of snapping about one thing or another with her, only made me long to claim her fully. I thought I could hold myself back while pleasuring her, but I suspected *I* might soon be the one begging.

In matings like ours, where our pendants chose, the woman fell in love with her male quickly. The male's heart followed, though I'd always believed he loved her for who she was, not solely because he desired her and vice versa. The pendant might choose, but the hearts made the final decision.

I liked Rhoslyn, and the tightness settling into my chest told me this liking could very easily tip into love.

Would that be a bad thing?

My mother had loved my father, and she was nearly broken when he set her aside to mate with another.

My situation was different. I'd watch and see where this went.

We passed a large building housing one of the many metalworking shops and paused to look through the large window on the front. This section of town was far enough from the water that the dresalods didn't reach.

"See?" I said loudly to project my voice above the bangs and shrieks of metal work echoing around us. "This is where we make the sheets we attach to the sides of our buildings."

Even outside the big open warehouse, the air was thick with a metallic scent—a tangy blend of hot iron and smoky coal that hung heavily in my nostrils. It tickled at the back of my throat.

Orcs struck hammers rhythmically, each filling the air with vibrations bouncing off worn stone walls and the exposed wooden beams above them.

Heat from roaring furnaces filtered through the glass, and flames flickered from the open doors of the enormous burners. Veins of white-hot fire bathed in blazing orange and pulsating yellow drew the eye. Molten globules cascaded toward sodden floors—their incandescent glow illuminating taut muscles flexing under orcs' firm grips on burning rods. As they worked, sparks danced around them. Sweat glistened on their brawny torsos covered only with sturdy leather aprons.

"It's amazing," Rhoslyn breathed, and since I could barely hear her, I took her hand and led her past the front of the building, continuing down the side road that looped around this part of the city and slowly approached my building.

We reached my house and went inside.

Rhoslyn put her clothing away inside the bureau, and I hovered near the door, admiring how she moved. She stroked the folded clothing a number of times before sighing and sliding the drawer shut.

She shot me a shy smile. "You said you have work to do this afternoon? I could make you something to eat first if you'd like. You bought a lot of food, and unless you'd like me to use some of the older food, I could make something with the new."

When she sashayed closer to me, stopping in front of me, her gaze traveled down my front. My cock, naturally, sprang to attention.

She didn't have to do anything but look at me to spark my mating fire. It roared through my veins, insisting I must soon claim her. My pendant followed, glowing brightly.

"I know what I'd like to eat." I bumped away from the wall and stalked right up to her.

She backed toward the bed, her gaze smoldering. "Oh you do, do you?"

"Very much so."

When I tumbled her down onto the bed and loomed over her, she cupped my shoulders and her lips parted.

I slowly bunched up her skirts, watching her face. I traced my fingers up her leg, and her thighs parted.

Fire roared through me, and there was nothing and no one that would keep me from satisfying my mate.

As a sigh of desire slipped from her throat, I claimed her mouth with my own.

CHAPTER 20
RHOSLYN

He kissed down my neck and tugged up my blouse, his fingertips tracing across my breasts.

"I thought you had work to do this afternoon," I said in a breathy voice. "That you didn't wish to waste time puttering around with me."

"I always have time for you, mate."

I'd like to think his words meant his feelings for me were deepening, but he'd made it clear they wouldn't for some time.

I'd be foolish to fall in love with my orc husband if he'd never feel the same.

He stroked his thumb up my crease, pausing at the bud at the top to rub. "Are you saying you wish for me to leave you immediately, tiny mate?"

If only I didn't adore him calling me that.

"Or should I linger?" His fingertip pushed my undergarment to the side and slipped inside me. "I don't want you wearing anything under your skirts."

"You want me to wander around town with nothing beneath them?"

"When we're here in our home," he conceded with a grumble. His fingers stroked through my wet folds.

I could either relax into his touch and let him do whatever he pleased with my body, or I could speak up every now and then. "I believe what I wear is my choice, orc mate."

He grinned up at me, his finger teasing inside my passage. "Call me that again."

Heat spread through me, making my skin tingle. My eyes rolled back in my head.

"Mate?" he prompted.

"Orc mate," I whispered.

"Yes, I'm your orc mate, and you, my pretty little human, like it when I touch you, don't you?"

He pumped his fingers inside me, and with each pull out, he dragged them over my bundle of nerves at the top, making me tremble.

Flames licked through me, creating a naughty feeling I couldn't seem to deny.

"It's midday," I gasped out. I braced my heels on the bed and lifted my hips up to meet the thrust of his fingers. "You shouldn't be doing this."

"Oh, believe me, tiny one. I should. And I've barely gotten started."

A slice of his thumb claw, and my only undergarment parted. He pulled his fingers out of me and left my clit throbbing, aching thing that it was.

I was.

Easing down, he stooped at the side of the bed. "Legs on my shoulders," he commanded, saying it in the demanding tone he might use with an underling. Damn, but my body wanted to melt all over him. He breathed on my core, and shivers tracked through me. I wanted everything, and it was all I could to not to beg. "Unless you'd prefer I go work in my office instead, my mate?"

If I didn't see a hint of vulnerability on his face when he looked up at me, I might've balked. Yes, my body throbbed for release, but I felt as if I waged a battle for my very soul. Unless I asserted myself when I could, he'd absorb everything that made me who I was as an individual. I also sensed if I stood up to him when it mattered most, he'd at least respect me.

"I'm doing this because I want to," I said, hooking my legs over his shoulders. "Not because you've teased my body to the point where it craves what you're doing."

"There's nothing wrong with wanting me."

"There is if it creates a power imbalance between us."

"I don't want anything but a partner." He dragged his thumb across my clit, and need shot through me.

"You weren't even looking for that a few days ago."

His crooked grin rose. "I am now."

And that was good enough for me.

"Lick me, Jaus," I said sternly.

"I live only to serve you, Rhoslyn." His mouth dropped to my clit, and my gasp rang out.

And when he pumped his fingers faster inside me, my world came apart.

Jaus gathered up the pieces of me and held them gently in calloused hands.

THE NEXT FEW days continued in the same pattern. I bathed him, he teasingly did the same, making my body explode each time. I prepared our meals, though he now insisted on cleaning the dishes after while I stood nearby, trying not to fret that he was doing something I should instead.

On my seventh day in the orc kingdom, we ate lunch like usual and he went to his office after. I puttered about the house, tidying this and that before finding some books in one of the wall cabinets in the bedroom. Since they were written in the universal language, I could read them.

Funny, a few looked like romances, but I had to be reading the titles incorrectly. One that looked like it discussed the local vegetation sounded interesting, so I tucked it beneath my arm.

Jaus had softened toward me, and if I cared to name it, he catered to my every need. He kept our home supplied with butter, fruit, and vegetables, things I'd noted weren't in the cool box when I first arrived. He tidied our home, and he insisted on preparing half our meals—while still cleaning everything after.

For a male who stated I was going to essentially be his housemaid, he seemed determined to do more than half my "job".

If only I felt useful for more than washing my clothing and making the bed in the morning.

With the book in hand, I curled up on the bed and read. So far, I refused to call the bedroom ours, though I suspected I wouldn't be able to hold out much longer. I was falling in love with my gruff, though gentle, orc mate, and there didn't seem to be anything I could do about it.

Even more, I *wanted* to fall for him, to care for him and give him the same pleasure he showed me.

The story I read was good, but my yawns caught up to me and I fell asleep, the book falling onto the bed beside me.

I woke with Jaus crawling over me.

"You're lovely when you sleep." The huskiness and hint of adoration in his voice were my undoing. I cupped his shoulders, holding on tight.

"You're not ugly when *you* sleep," I quipped. This wasn't exactly asserting myself so much as showing him I wasn't a lump of clay he'd found in the stream, intending to mold it.

"I'm blisteringly handsome." He shoved the book off

the bed and tugged at my skirts. "And you, my pretty one," He planted a kiss on my nose, "are much too distracting."

"You came to the bedroom. I didn't stroll into your office and putter around you to gain your attention."

"You can do so at any time." His lips curled up on one side. "I think I'd like to suck on your clit while you recline on my desk."

Shivers of need seared across my skin.

"Did you have any plans this afternoon?" It was all I could do to speak normally. "Evening, actually, since late-day sunlight is slanting through the room."

"My only task this early evening is to show my Rhoslyn what she's missing out on."

"I don't believe I'm missing out on much."

"I refer to my equally handsome cock."

"I'm not sure any cock is handsome. They're veiny and thick and the skin shifts across them when they're touched."

"How do you know so much about cocks?" His fingertip paused just inside my entrance and his thumb stopped circling my clit.

I wanted to jerk my hips up to impale myself with his finger. As always, my resolve was rapidly fading, and I sensed it wouldn't be long before I demanded he give me all he had to offer.

Love for him had stomped its way into my heart almost from the moment I met him. He irked me so much. Teased me unmercifully.

And despite snapping at him, I loved being with him.

"I'm not a maiden," I said, my voice throaty and husky. "As I pointed out to you already."

His finger plunged inside me, and he shifted it around, stroking my inner walls. "Experience is a good thing. I don't need to worry so much that I'll hurt you."

"How could you hurt me?"

He pumped his finger faster, adding another while rubbing my clit. "I'm big."

"I imagine you'll find a way to fit it inside me."

His eyebrow quirked up, making my pulse surge. "Would you like a sample?"

"You're saying I don't need to beg?"

He grumbled. "That was a tease. I didn't truly mean it."

"I believe you *did* mean it." How was I finding the wits to speak? My body kept coiling tight and releasing, and each time it tightened, everything inside me threatened to shatter.

"Perhaps I did at first, but I no longer do."

What was I going to do with that information? The thought that his feelings had changed for me, that he might one day love me, made me ache to confess how dear he was to me already. What if he told me he'd never feel the same?

Grr. I didn't like thinking this way. He showed me with each gesture and touch that I meant something to him. That was enough—for now.

"Come mate," he said. "I want to taste your pleasure

on my tongue." Spreading my legs wide, he crawled between them. "Give me everything."

And when he placed his mouth on my feverish flesh, I did as he asked.

CHAPTER 21
JAUS

"Would you like something to eat?" Rhoslyn asked after we'd bathed and I'd satisfied her again. My poor cock throbbed, but I could ignore it. The only thing that mattered to me now was giving her complete satisfaction. "I believe we have some grilled meat in the cool box."

Her easy smile told me I'd pleased her once more. By bringing her to orgasm over and over with my fingers and mouth, she didn't need my cock. Or she felt she didn't need my cock. She was not a maiden, and I didn't care one way or the other about that. As I said, at least she knew what to expect.

Did she realize my cock could make this even better? Despite her mocking me for my arrogance when we first met, I hadn't been thinking of things that way. But surely a cock pumping in and out of her would feel even better than my fingers.

I hoped I'd soon find out. The longer I went without claiming her, the more I ached to do so.

She meant . . . a lot to me. That was all I was prepared to admit to myself. I needed to remain detached at my core until I'd achieved the goals I'd set for myself when my mother moved away from my father and into her own estate. I'd be the best commander this city had ever seen, proving to everyone I was worthy.

The horns sounded outside.

Rhoslyn's wide-eyed gaze met mine.

"Dresalods," I snarled, rushing to grab my mace from the wall. I'd trained Feyla to come to my home whenever the alarm was given.

"You said they only come every month or so."

"Their patterns have been changing. Sometimes, they attack more often."

She rushed across the living area as I removed the bar and opened the inner door. "Come back to me, Jaus."

The heavy emotion in her voice was my undoing. I tugged her close and held her, praying she'd be safe— that *I'd* also be safe—at the end of the attack.

Finally, I had to go. She looked up at me with so much emotion in her eyes, my heart stalled. I floundered, knowing I needed to leave, that my fellow orcs needed me, but wanting so much to sit on the sofa and just hold her.

"Go. I'll bar the door and wait for you." She blinked fast, and it stunned me that she might be crying for me.

I stroked my knuckles down her face and left,

striding down the hall. Once she'd barred the first door behind me, I opened the outer panel and stepped outside, finding Feyla waiting.

One leap, and I landed on her spine, guiding her into the sky and toward the sea.

When we coasted past the wall, I frowned.

No dresalods?

"Where are they?" I called to the head of the guard.

"False alarm." He had the grace to wince. "One of my males thought he saw a few leaving the sea further down the coast. He flew here fast and sounded the alarm, but when we sent a flight to battle, they didn't find even one dresalod."

"Very well." Spent adrenaline made my limbs ache. With a nudge of my heels, I turned Feyla, and urged her back to my home. She landed on the balcony, and I dismounted.

After stroking her neck, I slapped her flank, urging her to return to her nest. I strode forward and tapped on the door.

Rhoslyn unbarred it. She burst out and rushed to me, sagging into my arms. "What's happening?"

I explained and took her inside where I gave into my earlier urge to hold her. She was rapidly becoming more important to me than anything, and I wasn't sure if I should give into the feeling or continue to fight it.

Finally, I set her on her feet and rose.

"Come, tiny mate, we'll eat in the city," I said, my

voice gruff with relief that I'd live to see another day with Rhoslyn.

Her head tilted. "We're leaving the house?"

"Tonight, we'll hold a festival to give thanks that everyone in the city still lives."

"Oh, that sounds fun."

The excitement in her voice made me realize other than buying clothing, I'd kept her inside our home. She was missing out on the other wonders of my city, and I wanted to share them with her.

"Wear something you can dance in," I said with a grin.

She trailed her fingertip down my arm as she passed me, heading for the bedroom. "Tell me more about this celebration."

I tugged on clean pants. "We hold them often." Because we knew each day could be our last. "The elders will hold a Flame Dance Festival where we'll light numerous majestic bonfires throughout the city. Street performers dressed in bright costumes will dance around them, as will we. Vendors will offer every kind of food you can imagine. The sparks from the fire filling the night sky represent not only celebration but will reinforce the unity within our society."

"It sounds amazing."

I couldn't wait to share it with her.

We finished dressing and left our home. Orcs walked with us, heading toward the city center.

I took Rhoslyn's hand to avoid losing her in the rush.

Color filled her cheeks, and her cheerful gaze took in everything. As we passed acrobats performing leaps and flips from the backs of others, her breath caught, and she squeezed my hand.

The sun faded, leaving only streaks of gold and red on the western horizon, and torches stuffed with fragrant herbs were lit. The buildings we passed were adorned with colorful tapestries depicting our victorious battles against the dresalods.

Dusk settled over the city, and the air was filled with anticipation.

"He looks a little like you," Rhoslyn said, pausing to stare at a tapestry.

I studied the picture of a dresalod lying in the middle of the square, an orc standing on top of its enormous shell, his mace lifted and a snarl on his face.

"I've been commander of the forces for a little over five years." I didn't want to sound like I was bragging.

"It *is* you? Wow." She stared at the picture once more, comparing it with me. "The artist did a good job. You don't look grumpy at all here."

My laugh snorted out, surprising both of us.

She grinned. "There you go again, turning into an orc who just might be a bit squishy inside."

"Never," I vowed with a growl.

But truly. Maybe? Only with Rhoslyn.

Tugging her forward, we made our way to the middle of city where we held the open-air market during the day. At night and after a dresalod battle, even if this one was thwarted, the area was given over to the party.

"The fire is huge." Rhoslyn gaped at the towering mound of logs taking up the center of the square.

As the flames flickered and cast a warm glow over the city, my heart pounded in sync with the mesmerizing beat of drums radiating through the air.

"The Flame Dance Festival has commenced," I said loudly by her ear.

It engulfed us in an atmosphere brimming with excitement and celebration.

Rhoslyn's wide eyes took in the vibrant dancers twirling like ethereal beings around the fire. Her hand tightened on mine, sharing this moment.

I smiled at her wonder-filled expression, seeing the celebration we'd held so many times in the past from her eyes. It was vibrant. Exciting. Just like her.

She turned toward me; her gaze reflecting both awe and admiration. "I never imagined such a sight could exist within the city."

Sparks painted patterns across a dark sky as we drew closer together. With an instinctive urge to protect her from any lurking danger, I tugged her into my arms and held her against my chest, my body serving as armor for hers.

We soaked up every detail of our surroundings. I wanted to etch this moment in my heart. It felt new and different—and wonderful—because I was spending this time with her.

A breeze swept through cobblestone pathways lined with stalls selling sweet delicacies, and a hint of a spice wafted past us, its scent mingling with the raw passion lingering between Rhoslyn and me.

I craved her like no other, and I suspected I'd feel this way about her until my dying day.

Curling around her, I kissed her flushed cheek.

The smile she sent me over her shoulder warmed me even more than the flames dancing in her animated eyes. A bond was forming between us that felt like an unbreakable thread weaving patterns across my heart.

Was I falling in love with her?

I must be and not only because we were mates chosen by my Azuris Clan.

I was falling in love with Rhoslyn for who she was. Her joy of each moment shone in her eyes and in her touch, and I wanted it directed at me.

Turning her in my embrace, I gently cupped her face, searching her gaze, hoping to find the same feelings expressed there. Did I? I thought so.

I kissed her, and her lips met mine eagerly. It was a kiss that celebrated victory while embodying so much more than mere physical touch.

Time seemed to stand still as I deepened the kiss. She pressed against me, moaning, her fingers fluttering against my chest.

I lifted my head, and when she looked up at me, I felt like I could conquer the world.

Orcs danced wildly around us, their movements

mimicking the battles we'd fought, plus those we have yet to engage in.

"Together," someone shouted, and others joined in shouting the same.

Rhoslyn turned in my arms, pressing back against me again. I held her hands, entwining our fingers, though mine were so much larger than hers, they essentially engulfed hers.

"We should dance too," she shouted over the roar of the crowd. "I want to dance until I'm spent, then keep going. You said the dance celebrates life, and we need to capture it while we still can."

She spoke what was in my heart each time we built another fire and gathered around it.

Initially, we only swayed, but soon, we moved as quickly and feverishly as those around us. I didn't let her out of my sight or beyond my arm's reach. The need to protect my mate drove me unlike any other.

We danced to show resilience.

Determination.

And each time we brushed together; our dance reflected our inner mate fire.

CHAPTER 22

JAUS

Finally I felt I couldn't put it off any longer.

The king would expect me to bring Rhoslyn to the palace and introduce her.

On our way there the next morning, I took her past the apothecary shop, pausing while keeping my expression neutral. She was a healer—I sensed she was a good one—and she longed to slip back into the role she'd chosen in her own village. Her skills would be welcome here.

When we stopped in front of the shop, I watched for her reaction.

"Do we have time . . .?" She gazed longingly through the open door. "I don't have any money, but can I look?"

"We can stop but only for a moment," I said gruffly, hiding my smile.

Disappointment clouded her face, and she nodded

quickly. "I don't want to keep you from your appointment with the king."

"I don't have an appointment, per se." I waved to the shop. "Enter. Please."

Inside, I followed her as she wandered down the rows between shelves filled to the brim with vials containing bright-colored liquids and sachets with various herbs. She kept picking one up, sniffing it, and shooting me a smile that faded quickly when she replaced the items on the shelf. Even this tiny bit of sadness gutted me. It made me want to give her the world.

The proprietor joined us, nodding both our ways. He held out a basket to Rhoslyn.

She shook her head. "We're just looking but thank you."

I carefully gestured to him, and he shot me a confused look before his expression cleared and he nodded.

"I recognize so many herbs," Rhoslyn said, weaving among the aisles with the proprietor following us. I shielded him from her view, and each time she sighed over a powder or what looked like clusters of sticks to me, I'd carefully gesture. He'd then collect whatever she'd admired and place it inside the basket.

"I could buy you a few things," I said carefully.

She touched my arm, though only briefly, and the soft look she sent me made my lungs freeze. "Maybe one or two. I wouldn't want to spend much. You work too hard for your coins."

I had more than I could ever spend. My mother's family had wealth, and they'd ensured my accounts overflowed before I fully matured.

Stopping, Rhoslyn gestured to a woven container full of dried grayish-green leaves. "Lindenmint. It makes a delicious tea. I used to drink at least one cup each morning. I love the flavor. It contains properties that keep the teeth clean, and I found it worked quite well as an astringent."

"Truly?" the older orc said. "I hadn't heard the last bit."

Her voice strengthened as she slipped back into her role as a healer. "Lindenmint, when ground finely and mixed with boiled water, then applied to a wound, slows the blood flow from even fairly deep cuts. I was quite convinced it had properties that fought infection as well, though I'd just begun to test it when I left the fortress for the Hunt."

"I suspect you're an amazing healer," I said, and the apothecary nodded, his eyes full of respect.

"The women in my family have served as healers for many generations. My mother taught me not only where to find and how to prepare what I collected, but how best to use them. She also taught me how to test something to discover new ways it might be used." She fingered a leaf, bringing it to her nose for a sniff that made her smile wistful. "I used to pick it each fall along the edge of the forest. My mother laughed at how much I'd collect, saying I'd be able to prepare tea for the entire village for a full winter, but she enjoyed it too, as did my father. The bushes are large. They're hearty and grow in almost any soil."

After she moved on, it only took one heavy look on my part to the older orc for him to scoop up a generous amount of the herb and place it in the basket.

"Do you have more?" I asked softly as Rhoslyn turned left at the end of the aisle.

"I do. It grows in the foothills of the mountain. It's easily obtained." He watched her with an indulgent smile. "Your mate has a vast knowledge of herblore. If she'd like a job—"

"She won't need to work for financial reasons, but I'll discuss it with her. She might want to meet with you to discuss herbs and remedies or help others to keep busy. I suspect she's bored when I work. You may learn from each other."

"I always welcome learning from someone new. You'll be surprised how the uses of what we collect varies depending on region and culture." He gave me a short bow. "I'd be honored to learn from your mate."

While Rhoslyn continued walking around, exclaiming over one herb or another, I paid for the items we'd collected.

The elder orc leaned close to me across the back counter. "She mentioned a tea. If you'd like, I'll make her a cup to take with you."

I braced his shoulder, my heart filled with gratitude. "Thank you."

"I'm done," Rhoslyn finally said, still gazing longingly at the shelves. "Do you think I could come back again someday? Smelling the herbs and potions reminds me of home."

"I'm sure that can be arranged." I kept my voice growly as she'd expect, but inside I smiled.

There were many ways to please my mate, and I was quickly discovering that making her happy was the only thing that mattered.

CHAPTER 23
RHOSLYN

We left the shop, and when Jaus paused, I did too.

Distant shouts drew my attention, but when I peered down both ends of the street, I didn't see any reason for the uproar. Perhaps it was just vendors hawking their wares in the central marketplace, their voices somehow amplified by the narrow street.

The older orc proprietor hurried out to join us. "You forgot your purchases." He handed me a big bag that Jaus promptly took from me to carry.

I shot a panicked look Jaus's way. He'd said I could get a few items, but this was much more than that. He was going to think I was greedy. "I didn't ask for so much."

"In some ways, you did." The indulgent smile Jaus sent me sunk into my bones and made me feel giddy. "I had the proprietor add a few extra items I thought you might enjoy."

"You have an indulgent mate," the older orc said, his cheeks spreading wide with his smile. "I took the liberty of preparing you a bit of lindenmint tea to sip as you stroll through town." He handed me the mug. "I placed a cover over the top to help hold in the heat." He demonstrated how the thick fabric lifted, revealing one side of the rim while continuing to cover the rest. "Drink, then cover it back up, and it'll remain piping hot until your last sip."

"Thank you so much." I gave him a hug, taking care not to jostle the tea, and when I stepped back, his face darkened.

"You're very welcome, my dear." His gaze sought Jaus's, who nodded. "If you'd like to stop by again sometime, we'll share a cup of tea and talk herbs. It's rare for me to find someone else who is as knowledgeable as you about their properties. I can learn from you and you from me. My name's Liall, by the way." He rubbed the side of his neck and shifted his shoulder-length, bluish-gray hair over his shoulder.

"Oh, I'm not sure—"

"Would a day next week work for you?" Jaus asked Liall.

Liall bowed to me. "I would make time for you any day of the week."

Jaus grunted. "Why don't we stop by in the afternoon on secondist? I'll meet with the leader of the guard team who mans the outer wall, something I've needed to take care of, and you, my mate, can sit and enjoy tea and herblore with Liall. If this is something you'd like to do."

"I would," I essentially gushed.

However, I wasn't sure what to think of this. For a male who made it clear he didn't want a bride, Jaus was treating me much too kindly. I wanted to give him a kiss of thanks, but I wasn't sure how he'd take it. This might just be a whim on his part.

"Secondist mid-afternoon, then," Liall said, bowing to me again. "It was a delight meeting you." He hurried back into his shop.

Because I couldn't resist, I tucked back part of the mug's cover and sipped the piping hot tea, sighing at how amazing it tasted. Liall had placed a tiny sachet with the herbs in the water and it would continue to steep.

"Good?" Jaus asked, gently stroking his knuckles down my cheek.

"Amazing." I might not dare give him a kiss, but I was happy to lean into his side and grin up at him. "If you're not careful, I'm going to start thinking you like me."

"I can't imagine not finding you appealing, tiny mate," he said gruffly. He sucked in a breath and shot it out, waving to the walkway lining the cobbled street. "Are you ready to continue?"

"Lead away," I said, my mood bubbling over. Our relationship might've started out with squabbling, but we'd turned a corner somewhere and were heading in an exciting direction.

He liked me!

Maybe soon, he might actually love me.

We strolled to the end of the street, where we turned onto a wider avenue. To the right, the street continued straight all the way to the southern edge of the city, meeting up with the outer wall. The briny smell in the air told me the sea must be in that direction.

Orcs rushed our way, but that was nothing new. I held onto my tea and backed against a shop wall with Jaus to wait for the bustling crowd to pass.

A few of them cried out, and my breath caught.

I shot Jaus a worried look, finding his attention trained to the southern end of the street, his fingers on the mace strapped to his back.

"I need you to go inside and hide near the back wall," he growled, pulling his mace. He turned and jostled the knob of the shop, but it wouldn't open, not even when he shoved his shoulder against it. His stricken gaze met mine, and he leaped a few steps over to try another door that also wouldn't open. He looked up but this section of town was filled with three- and four-story buildings made up of smooth silver. "Up." He dropped his mace and lifted me, but the second level window was too high and out of my reach. Cursing, he urged me into a shallow nook between one shop and another. I barely fit. "Stay there. Don't draw attention."

"What's going on?" I didn't like that the street was now deserted, the orcs running through it having fled.

A screech rang out, echoed by another. The fear roaring through my veins told me I knew that sound.

Dresalods.

Jaus grabbed his mace and looked down at me, his gaze full of an emotion I couldn't define. He stroked my cheek with his knuckles. "Tiny mate. Please stay safe."

With a growl, he pivoted and strode out into the middle of the empty street, facing three of the enormous creatures.

They shrieked and scrambled toward him.

JAUS

My mate was in danger, and all I could think of was protecting her.

With a thunderous roar, the first dresalod lunged at me, its massive pincers snapping the air. If it grabbed my arm, it would sever it with one click. Adrenaline surged through my veins as I sidestepped its initial assault, narrowly avoiding being skewered by its wickedly sharp claws. Time seemed to slow around me as I planned my counterattack.

Swinging my mace in an arc above my head, I brought it crashing down on the creature's front limbs with all my might. A deafening crack echoed through the street as exoskeleton met metal, but I failed to break through entirely. Undeterred, I pressed on by stepping back before delivering a blow directly into another vulnerable joint.

The sound was sickening—like shattering glass

mingled with crunching gravel—as fragments of chitin and flesh sprayed outward from where I made contact. The beast shrieked in fury while thrashing violently on the cobbled street.

Swift movement caught out of the corner of my eye sent me spinning—another dresalod charged toward where my precious mate stood trembling, her cup of lovely tea held up as it might serve as a weapon.

With lightning reflexes honed through countless battles won on split-second decisions, every muscle fiber in my body surged into action once again.

I flung myself upward, curling and rolling over the beast, landing squarely between it and Rhoslyn.

She yelped my name but remained in place.

I'd sacrifice myself to keep her safe.

Ducking beneath the frenzied snap of the creature's front claw, time appeared to slow. With two hands gripping the hilt, I swung my mace, driving it partway through the beast's side. It staggered to the right, and I followed, determined to end its life and eliminate the third. Were there more? A quick glance told me no—so far. Perhaps the wall guard hadn't been mistaken when he said he saw dresalods to the south. Somehow, a few had slipped past our wall and remained hidden until they felt it was the right time to attack.

With a shriek, the creature I fought scrambled toward the gate at the end of the street, determined to escape to the sea.

I leaped onto its back, nearly toppling off when it

bucked, and hefted my mace. I brought it down hard on the dresalod's head, and it staggered, falling forward. I rode with it, jumping off when it crashed to the ground.

With sweat pouring down my brow, I spun, my mace lifting.

The final dresalod rushed toward Rhoslyn.

I was too far away to reach her in time, but I raced toward her with determination driving my muscles and the strength of a legion of orcs firing my blood.

The stench of its rancid breath filled the air, mixing with the salty tang of the nearby sea.

With a thunderous roar, the dresalod lunged toward my tiny mate. I couldn't reach her in time!

Its front claw smacked against the silver wall near her head, and she gulped and leaned in the other direction. It kept poking, gouging toward the narrow space where she hid.

There wasn't enough room in the nook for her to slide out of its reach. Once the creature hit her, it would pluck her from the hole like a treat to be savored. Her life would be over in a flash.

I'd lose the only woman I'd ever love.

The power of a thousand orcs snarled inside me as I raced toward the dresalod, my mace already swinging.

Rhoslyn flung the mug full of tea at the beast, and it reeled back, screaming. It spiraled on its hind legs, its front claws snapping at the sky.

Tumbling onto its back, it scrambled the air with its spiked legs, shrieking over and over.

I grabbed Rhoslyn's arm and pulled her from the tiny gap between the buildings, tucking her behind me.

The dresalod flipped over and sprung to its feet.

Its body steamed and it spun in a circle before righting itself. Leaving us, it raced down the street, aiming for the outer wall, though it appeared sluggish. I gave chase, my heart on fire with determination to end this.

Leaping, I landed on the cobblestones behind it and used my momentum to swing my mace, bringing it crashing down on the creature's back with all my might. A deafening crack echoed through the street as bone met metal. My mace sunk in easily, a nice change.

As soldiers rushed toward us to give aid, the dresalod dragged itself away from me, its blood oozing onto the cobblestones. It struggled to reach the wall, though it appeared too injured to make its way up and over the side.

Its body still steamed. It flopped on the ground and twitched before it stopped moving. One final blow with my mace ended its life.

Spinning on my heel, I bellowed Rhoslyn's name.

She lay on the cobblestones unmoving, bright red blood leaching from a puncture wound in her thigh.

CHAPTER 25
JAUS

Bright red blood, so different from my orc gold, gushed from the puncture wound on Rhoslyn's leg. About the size of her fist, the hole exited on the back of her thigh. The claw had cut right through her leg.

She'd bleed to death if I didn't get her to a healer immediately.

While the soldiers made sure the dresalods were dead, I lifted her as gently as I could.

"Hold on, tiny mate," I hissed, trying not to jostle her as I moved quickly through the streets.

She didn't respond.

"Rhoslyn? Speak to me. Please."

Her eyelids fluttered, but they didn't open. A scrape on her left temple held the shadow of a growing bruise. Had she hit her head while trying to escape the dresalod?

"Wake, mate," I whispered desperately, but she didn't respond.

I was rushing down one of the streets that would eventually take me to the healer's residence when I ran into someone coming from the opposite direction.

A growl ripped up my throat. "Out of my way—"

"Is that how you should talk to your brother?" Madr asked with a grin that faded fast when he took in Rhoslyn slumped in my arms. He gaped at the wound in her thigh. "This is your mate. What—?"

"Dresalods attacked."

His eyes widened and he hefted the flail he always carried with him, just as I did my mace. "Where?"

"I killed them. Three, and there didn't appear to be others but the soldiers will look for them. They must've somehow slipped inside the city."

"I'll see if I can find out where," he said grimly.

"Rhoslyn's wounded. I have to get her to the healers before . . ." I didn't want to think about what might happen to this precious being.

"Take her to the palace." Madr braced my shoulder in support. "Place her in the cream suite and put pressure on the wound until I can bring the court healer to her."

With a nod, I left him, turning right at the corner and running toward the sea.

Beyond the outer gate to the palace, the broad area between the enormous building and the rest of the city was made up of a large courtyard full of flower gardens, paths, and fountains.

The other side of the palace faced the sea. Those walls had yet to be breached by dresalods, though if a few reached the top, the elite guard would destroy them. And the bars across the windows kept the creatures out. They'd find no entrance at the roof either, since it was equally seamless and made of smooth metal the staff regularly greased. Let them cling to the flags jutting up from the top of the towers and wail as we shoot them down with steel-tipped arrows.

The guards swept open the gate, nodding as I passed. Madr was the heir to the throne. If he didn't openly call me brother, they might've barred my way even though I commanded the army.

My father only allowed me entrance when the whim struck him. I hadn't been raised here or in the larger castle in the mountains. When the king told my mother to leave, that he was mating with another, she took me to her home her parents left her in the foothills of the mountains where she'd grown up. When she was killed by the shaydes, the estate became mine.

I raced across the open stretches of lawn, leaping over flowerbeds, and took the stairs to the main entrance three at a time. Rushing toward the stately carved wooden doors, I smacked my shoulder into one before the guard could hurry forward and swing it open.

Inside the foyer, I ignored the urgent calls of the guards and rushed up the stairs, taking them as fast as I could.

"Send Mastivule to the cream room," I shouted to the

head of the guards as I reached the first landing and started up the next flight of stairs.

"As you will, Commander," one of the guards called after me. "I'll see to it right away."

"Bring the medical cabinet to the room immediately as well," I added as I rounded another landing and continued to the third floor. "Madr will bring the court healer."

"I will see it done right away, sir!"

I twisted the doorknob to the cream suite and hurried inside. When I laid Rhoslyn gently on the bed, she didn't move or make a sound. I pressed my ear against her chest and was grateful to hear her strong heartbeat.

What would I do if I lost her?

I couldn't dwell on that now. Rushing to one of the bureaus, I pawed through the clothing intended for whichever guest might stop by and spend the night, tugging out a tunic. Everything was new and had never been used.

After tearing the shirt into strips, I wrapped one around her thigh above the wound and tightened it.

The flow of blood slowed to a trickle. Had the claw severed something vital inside my mate's leg?

In the adjoining bathing room, I saturated strips of tunic with icy water in the sink, running back to the room with them leaving a dripped trail behind me.

My tiny mate lay too still on the bed.

"In the name of the Azuris Clan, I claim you." Why

hadn't I spoken the sacred words the moment I met her? I was too stubborn, too stupid.

I could only hope I wasn't also too late.

Shaking off the fear clambering through me, I gently rolled her onto her side and tugged up her skirt, pressing one of the saturated strips against the underside of her wound. I eased her onto her back, maintaining pressure on her thigh while lying another strip against the front. It wasn't much, but if I could slow the blood flow, I'd give her a chance of survival.

Mastivule rushed into the room, waving for staff orcs to place the medicine cart near the head of the bed.

"The healer will be here shortly." After a long look at Rhoslyn, Mastivule grunted. "May the fates be with her." He touched a fingertip to his lips and tapped his brow before he and the guards left the room.

The door banged open, and Madr strode into the room with an older orc following. I was grateful to see Arkest, the eldest and most revered healer, with my brother.

Arkest gave me a nod and rushed to the side of the bed. "Your mate?"

"Yes, can you help her?" My voice cracked with pain. "Please."

"I will do my best." His rheumy gaze shot to my right arm. "After I tend to her, I'll suture that slice in your arm."

A glance showed a long cut angling along the muscle

that still bled, though not as profusely as Rhoslyn's leg. I hadn't noticed I was injured.

"It's nothing."

Arkest frowned. "Do you wish to lose the use of your dominant arm, Commander?"

"Help my mate." I gripped the foot of the bedframe tightly, and a cracking sound rang out.

Madr placed his hand on my shoulder. "Leave her to Arkest. He'll save your mate."

He tried to urge me away from the bed, but I shrugged him off. "I'll remain with Rhoslyn."

"I doubt she'll know you're here," Arkest said. He examined the mark on her forehead and clicked his tongue against the roof of his mouth. "This would explain why she's unconscious." He frowned at me. "If there's bleeding in her brain, she may not ever wake again."

"Do. Everything. You. Can," I growled. The bedframe split beneath my fingers.

"You distract me." Arkest's lips thinned. "Either remain silent or go away. Leave me to heal your mate. You won't help her by collapsing the bed beneath her."

I pried my fingers off the wooden frame but remained where I was, watching intently as Arkest loosened the binding I'd wrapped around her thigh above the wound.

"Good job," Arkest said, his voice lightening. "All that military training paid off."

"It also paid off when I killed the three dresalods who

attacked us on the street."

"As you should." Arkest lifted his hand, and his assistant wheeled the cart now holding a basin full of steaming water closer to the bed. He removed soft cloths from the medicine cabinet and waved for his assistant to lay his basket of herbs on the bed.

"My mate is a healer," I said.

Arkest didn't look up from where he carefully washed Rhoslyn's wound. "Interesting."

"We visited the herbalist today and my mate spoke of the properties of lindenmint."

"Freshens the breath and protects the teeth, but I don't see why you've chosen to speak of this unless you need a distraction—one our high prince has offered, and you should accept so you stop bothering me."

"She said she discovered it has astringent properties."

Arkest's hands froze over her leg. "I hadn't heard that before."

"Could you place the herb on her wound?" Somehow, I hadn't lost our purchases at the apothecary. I laid the bag on the bed, opening the top and pulling out the pouch of lindenmint. "There's no harm in trying is there?" I cringed as blood continued to trickle from her wound. "She's bleeding. If this can slow the flow, we should use it."

"Pressure and the tourniquet you wisely used are the best means of slowing blood flow short of suturing a torn artery. I don't believe this is arterial bleeding, however. It isn't squirting but flowing at a steady pace. Venous, if I had to guess, which I often must do."

"Let's try some on your arm," Madr said. "On that gash you dismissed that continues to seep and splatter on the floor."

Before I could say anything, he plucked a clump of lindenmint from the pouch and pressed it against my wound. A short moment later, he lifted it away.

"You're no longer bleeding, brother," Madr said in amazement.

"It's the lindenmint. Please." I'd do anything to get Arkest to listen. My poor mate continued to bleed. How could such a tiny being survive if she lost that much blood? Her pale face told me she might not—not unless we could stop the flow.

"I'm not opposed to trying lindenmint," Arkest said, following Madr's lead. "I'll grind it first and add boiled water, however, to make a poultice, not just stuff a clump of leaves against the wound." He twisted his lips as he gazed at my arm, before turning back to Rhoslyn.

In no time, he'd made the poultice and laid it over her wounds. "I don't wish to push it inside. We don't know what else this herb might do, and now is not the time for testing." His gaze caught mine. "But if this works, your mate may very well have saved herself."

"She said she's also noted lindenmint helps prevent infection."

Arkest grunted. "Now *that* would be truly amazing."

He secured a bandage to the front of the wound, and

we carefully rolled her, holding her in place while he tended to the exit wound in the same manner.

Even when we laid her on her back again, she didn't wake up.

What if I lost her? I couldn't bear the thought. I'd held back the words that would show her the feelings growing in my heart, because I felt my career and proving my worth was more important.

Would I be given time to show her how much she'd come to mean to me?

All I could do was beg the fates to grant my plea. *Heal her. Give me the chance to show her I . . .*

That I loved her.

There was no denying the feeling. My tiny mate had stolen my heart almost from the moment I met her.

If she lived, I'd do all I could to show her everything I'd held back from her.

"I'll stop by later, and then again tomorrow if there's need," Arkest said. "As for her head wound, there isn't anything we can do about that. Now we wait." He gathered his things and stepped away from the bed, his soft gaze lingering on Rhoslyn.

She breathed still. She slept. I had to trust that rest would heal her.

"Wait for what?" Madr asked from the foot of the bed. He shot me a look full of concern.

"We wait to see if she'll awaken or . . ." Arkest's grim gaze met mine.

Without finishing the thought, he left the room.

CHAPTER 26

RHOSLYN

Nightmares chased me, but each time a dresalod came near, Jaus's soft, soothing voice and the touch of his fingers on my face drove the creature away. My brave, strong mate would protect me. He'd killed the attackers and rescued me on the street. He'd chase them through my nightmares too.

Whenever I cracked open my eyes, I found him sitting beside me, holding my hand. I could swear he laid with me once, his arms wrapped around me, and his face cratered with grief.

"Please," he'd whispered many times and, "Tiny mate."

Then the dresalods would attack again, sucking me back into a world full of terrifying creatures surrounding me.

Shaydes haunted me as if I lived in endless night.

My leg burned through it all, and I thrashed, heat

scorching through me. My body would soak with sweat that someone would gently wash away.

Jaus bathed me, or I thought it was him. His was the only voice I heard, and his touch was already familiar. Welcome.

Once, I bolted upright, and he cupped my face, forcing me to meet his eyes. "It's alright, mate. You're safe. This I promise."

"Jaus," I murmured, my fear shifted aside by his gentle touch.

He eased me onto the soft surface and held me, kissing my brow and murmuring words in a language I didn't understand but found incredibly calming.

"You will live," he said over and over. "I will *not* allow you to die."

He was so strong and determined, I had no choice but to believe him. I clung to him, clung to his words.

And I finally slept.

I woke lying on incredibly soft bedding with someone stroking my face. The muted murmur of voices swam in and out of focus.

"You were wise to insist on a lindenmint poultice," someone said in a deep voice. "It worked, and I'll pass on the word to the other healers. Lindenmint grows every-where. To think we never discovered this property and only believed it was a simple tea."

"She's wise," someone else said. "You've chosen well brother."

"The fates and my clan chose, and I will thank them every day," Jaus said.

I couldn't seem to make my mind grab onto the world and keep me in it. When I shifted on the soft surface, a dull ache throbbed in my right thigh. I stilled; worried further movement would make my leg hurt even more.

The memory of the dresalods attacking us in the street rushed through me. While Jaus battled two, the third came after me. It kept trying to kill me. I'd dodge to the side as much as I could, but it hit me. My leg!

"When I first began my career," the older voice said, "I tested everything. The enthusiasm for my chosen profession drove me to explore the world around me." His clipped words came out with purpose. "As I aged, that feeling waned. I enjoyed my career, but I lost the wonder of discovery. I stopped testing, and I see now that I was wrong. I'm sorry I doubted you for even a moment."

"I bear you no ill will," Jaus said.

I remembered trying to press myself tighter into the nook between the buildings but being unable to sink deep enough to keep the creature from hurting me. It stabbed, hitting the wall around me over and over. I couldn't hide.

"Thank you," Jaus said. "I appreciate your help."

Footsteps echoed in the room, followed by a door opening and closing.

"She'll wake completely," the other person said from farther away. "I trust the fates wouldn't give her to you only to steal her not long after."

"She's incredibly smart," Jaus said. "Resourceful. I don't know what I'd do without her."

No, that couldn't be my grumpy mate speaking highly of me, his voice cratering with pain. If I could open my eyes, I would find out what was hurting him and make it go away. But I didn't dare invite the pain to stab through me again.

"She's . . . gorgeous," someone else said. "You're lucky, brother. Incredibly fortunate."

"The fates gave me a wonderful gift."

"Your clan is worthy. *You* are worthy, brother."

Brother? Jaus said he was an only child.

"My mother believed I was," Jaus said in a wry voice. "You know what my father thinks."

"He's a fool who'll never change his ways."

"If only what he thought of me didn't matter."

Poor Jaus. He hadn't mentioned his father, but it sounded like the guy scorned him. If I could get off this bed, I'd track his father down and smack him, tell him he should notice how wonderful—how loveable—Jaus was.

It had been so easy to fall deeply in love with him. His kind, gentle ways overrode his gruff, grumbly demeanor, showing me he *was* a cinnamon roll on the inside. He was strong and brave. He'd give his life to save others.

I sucked in a breath and tried to move again, finding it easier this time. Even better, my eyelids responded to my command and opened.

Jaus stood at the end of the bed beside a male orc about his own age. I'd never seen him before. He was as handsome as my mate, and I could tell by the shape of his jaw and their similar build that they were brothers.

The darkness beyond the windows taking up the left wall told me it was night. One of the windows had been cracked open, and the rich tangy scent of the sea drifted through the room, mixing in with what smelled like a subtle perfume and liladek flowers. Liladek only bloomed at night, and their blossoms could be used as a sleeping potion.

How long had *I* been asleep?

I had no idea where I was, but this wasn't Jaus's simple yet lovely home. How had I wound up in what looked like a bedroom fit for a queen?

They'd placed the magnificent bed I lay in—a grand four-poster draped with rich burgundy curtains that cascaded to the floor—in the center of the room. Its intricately carved wooden frame hinted at craftsmanship fit for royalty.

The plush mattress beneath me supported me like a cloud, and I was covered with layers of soft blankets in deep shades of gold and cream. Delicate lace pillows supported my head, and I couldn't imagine owning a room like this nor spending my nights lying in such splendor.

The bureaus standing by the right wall were made of a dark polished wood and crafted with elegant details mirroring those seen on the rest of the furniture scattered around the space like precious jewels.

Wood flooring gleamed between thick rugs in muted cream—something I'd hate to have to keep clean. Portraits of stately orcs peppered the walls, their stern gazes looking my way.

When I caught his eye, utter relief filled Jaus's face, making my pulse dance through my veins. He quickly rounded the side of the bed and crouched down beside it, taking my hand, his intent gaze remaining locked on mine. "How are you feeling, tiny mate? Better?"

The other male watched us with a smile twitching his lips upward.

"Weak. I remember the dresalods attacking and you killing them all."

"I'd kill a legion to protect you, my little one."

If only I dared read more into his statement. Caring and kindness were all well and good, but I wanted more.

I'd fallen in love with my husband just like he'd predicted. Would he ever feel the same way about me?

"I was wounded," I said.

"How's your leg? You had a fever, and you've been unconscious for three days."

"What?" I started to sit up, and he helped me, supporting my back while he fluffed soft pillows behind me.

"We consulted the best healers, naturally," the other

male said. "By the way, it's nice to finally meet you, sister." His grin widened as he looked back and forth between us. "I'm thrilled that Jaus's hunt was successful."

"This is my half-brother, Madr," Jaus said, his attention remaining on me.

"You wouldn't happen to have a sister, would you?" Madr asked. "One who might be persuaded to race through the woods, though not too fast, because I suspect I'd like to catch her." Madr's low chuckle made my pulse flip.

He was devastatingly handsome, though not as gorgeous as my mate.

"I do have a sister," I croaked. After a deep swallow, my voice cooperated better. "But she loves another and will soon wed."

Madr grinned easily. "Ah, well, it was worth asking. Good for her. Bad for me."

"Where am I?" I asked.

"The royal family's seaside palace," Madr said. "It's rarely used. You're welcome to stay here for as long as you'd like."

"Palace?"

"I brought you here after you were wounded," Jaus said. "The court healer tended to you himself."

"Is everyone else alright? Was anyone harmed by the dresalods?"

"Jaus, here," Madr patted his brother's back, "took

care of the latest dresalod problem before it could turn into a menace. Fortunately, no one else was hurt."

I tried to fathom what must've happened after the dresalods attacked. Would we get into trouble for coming here? Although, Jaus was the commander of the orc military. Perhaps he was welcome here and me, by association.

"It's nice of the . . . royal family to let me stay here while I recover," I said. "We can leave if we've overstayed our welcome."

Madr chuckled, and his sparkling gaze met Jaus's. "You can stay here forever if you'd like. As I said, the palace is rarely used, and there are twenty-seven rooms. I suspect someone could stay in this room, and the staff would never realize they were here."

None of this made sense.

Jaus cleared his throat and shot his brother a wry look. "I need to mention that Madr is the heir to the orc kingdom."

"At your service, sister," Madr said with a low bow.

Brother. Heir to the orc kingdom. Was Madr a *prince?* If so, did that mean Jaus was royal as well?

My eyes widened.

Madr continued to chuckle, savoring this reveal. Why hadn't Jaus told me?

"My mother and father were not mated," Jaus hurried to say. "Madr will assume the throne when our father chooses to step aside."

"Which won't be for a very long time," a sharp voice said from the open doorway across the very large room.

An older, grim-faced orc male with broad shoulders and a narrow waist strode over to stand beside Madr at the foot of the bed. He wore a tunic adorned with gold on the cuffs and around the helm, plus a golden signet across his brow.

"Well," he said with a sneer, his heavy gaze jerking down my frame. "Is this your puny human mate, Jaus?"

CHAPTER 27

RHOSLYN

"This is my *lovely* human mate," Jaus said sharply, straightening. He was taller than his father, though about the same height as Madr. The only resemblance between them could be found in the shape of their jawline and nose, plus the dark golden color of their eyes.

Madr's eyes had the green cast I'd found common in orcs. Like his father, his hair was tinted with green. Perhaps he got his eye color from his mother.

"This is Madr's father," Jaus said in a hollow voice, his gaze not leaving the older male. "King Surled."

Should I rise and bow—no, curtsy—to the king?

As if he understood my thought, Jaus gave me a negative jerk of his head.

Alright, I'd lie here. It wasn't like I trusted using my leg yet anyway.

"*Our* father," Madr grated out.

The king snorted.

So, he was the one who'd hurt Jaus—the one I wanted to smack. I sent him a glare that should impale him on the spot, but he didn't even flinch.

Like my husband, I wouldn't refer to him as anything but my new liege lord. Mine only because I would remain here in the kingdom with Jaus.

Madr shook his head. "You can acknowledge him, Father. Everyone knows."

"I've done all I should," King Surled said with a twist of his brow. "He's commander of my military, is he not?"

"A position he earned with his sweat and leadership. A position that could see him killed," Madr grumbled. "How will you ensure your line if something should happen to me? Acknowledge my brother. Then, any orclings he has with his new mate will be accepted as part of the family."

"Half-orclings." The twist of King Surled's face told me he didn't welcome my children any more eagerly than Jaus's. "*You're* not the commander of my military, Madr. You'll remain safely behind the walls until you find a mate and plant numerous orclings in her body."

"I'm not safe *anywhere* inside the kingdom. My brother proved that three days ago when he killed the dresalods who must've hidden inside an empty building, waiting for the right opportunity to attack."

I still had a hard time believing I was unconscious for three days.

"And whose fault is that?" The king drilled Jaus with his heavy gaze.

"They breed too fast and are too eager to hunt us," Madr said. "I've told you many times we need to find a way to eliminate them permanently, not wait around to fight off each attack."

"Then speak with my advisors. See if you can help them dream up something." King Surled's attention fell on me again, and from his growing sneer, I got the idea I would not be remaining here to recover for long.

"It's nice of you to stop to check on my welfare," I said smoothly, holding back the mockery I longed to include in my voice.

The king pivoted on his heel and strode from the room without saying a word.

"He's warming up to the idea," Madr told Jaus.

Anger brewed in Jaus's eyes. "He's not."

I wanted to hug him and tell him I adored him, but I sensed what he needed most would not come from me. But I also suspected he wasn't waiting for his father to acknowledge him. That he'd refuse to become an official part of the royal family even if the king held out his arms. Jaus appeared to enjoy living a simple life, and so did I.

"We need to leave." I flung back the blankets, noting I wore a lacy nightgown and bit back my somewhat giddy laugh. Jaus told Eleri I didn't need any nighties, and at the time, my pulse shot through the roof. Then, I'd pictured us in his bed, completely naked. Entwined. Giving each other pleasure.

"You can't leave," Madr said. "You need to rest." He huffed at Jaus, who returned to the side of the bed and scooped me up in his arms.

I was certain I could walk, but it felt wonderful to be held by my mate. I wasn't going to protest. Besides, my feet were bare. I couldn't walk through town like that.

Madr concerned gaze fell on me. "Sister, I only want you safe."

"I appreciate your kindness, Madr, and in return for your favor, you should come to dinner one night at Jaus's home. I'll prepare you a nice meal."

Madr's lips twisted, but he relented, shooting me a grin that would make every woman on the planet swoon if they saw it. "I'd like that."

He was the opposite of their father, sweet and generous. One day, he'd make a fine king.

"Thank you for letting us come here." Jaus strode across the room with me in his arms. I clung to his shoulders and pressed my ear against his broad chest to listen to his heartbeat.

It raced, and I hoped it did so because he was near to me.

CHAPTER 28

JAUS

Madr followed us down three flights of stairs to the enormous front foyer.

"Don't you want to eat something before you go?" he asked when I paused.

"Thank you, but we have food at my home." Despite my urge to snap and snarl after my encounter with my supposed father, I held in my irritation. I loved my brother, and I didn't want to take my anger out on him. "My mate will recover best in her own bed." *My* bed. I'd pamper her and indulge her every whim.

I'd nearly lost her, and I refused to hold myself back from her any longer.

"You're sure?"

My brother loved me; he had from the day we met when I was three and him a toddling orcling of one year old. His mother named me as his older brother. My father's mate had been his polar opposite: sweet, kind, and welcoming even to her husband's bastard orcling.

If only she wasn't murdered during the big shayde attack along with my mother and childhood friend. Madr and I had mourned together, growing even closer.

"Come share a meal with us in a few days," I said, striding toward the front door. "I should've invited you sooner."

"I will." Madr scrunched his lips. "Let me at least call a coach for you."

"I can carry my tiny mate."

"Very well." He gestured for two of the six guards flanking the enormous front doors to open them, and they did so immediately. "Two, follow."

When I met his steely gaze, I knew better than to argue. He'd send protection with us, and nothing I said would dissuade him.

I nodded my thanks. I couldn't hold Rhoslyn and properly defend her.

I stepped outside onto the broad stone platform. More guards looked our way, though they remained at their stations.

Madr joined us outside. His gaze fell on Rhoslyn. "I envy you, brother."

His pendant should've brightened during the Hunt, not mine. Not that I would want anyone but me to claim Rhoslyn, but he was a decent person and so worthy of love.

"Thank you for everything." With a nod, I carried my tiny mate down the stairs, across the large courtyard, and out through the gate.

RHOSLYN

"I can walk," I said as he strode through the streets, his long stride eating up the distance. Whenever anyone came near us, he released a low growl, and they backed away, their hands lifting.

Two guards remained well behind us, their weapons pulled and their sharp gazes scanning the area.

"I enjoy carrying you," Jaus said.

"Your arms must be tired."

"*You* must be tired."

"From what I just learned; I've slept for three days. You'd think I'd be perky by now." Instead, I felt worn out. Heartsick if I chose to name it, and not for myself. "When my leg's all better, I want to go back to the palace and kick the king."

Jaus's low chuckle tickled across my bones, and I was relieved to feel his shoulders loosen beneath my palms. "He wouldn't take that kindly."

"He deserves it and much more. I'd be tempted to smack him as well."

"If it helps, I've kicked him myself a few times, though not for many years."

"I hope you kicked him hard."

His smile shone down on me, so sweet and gentle that it made my heart hurt. "I've been a tough thing from the time I was small."

He would have to be with such a horrible father.

"We won't see him again," Jaus said.

"We don't need to."

"He's always aware of what I do, and I never know why."

"It's hard to understand family, isn't it?"

"He's never given me any reason to believe he cares if I live or die."

His soft words just about killed me. I leaned my head against him, tightening my arms around his neck. How could I show him how wonderful he was?

"The king came to my room," I said. "He met me."

"That was his curiosity getting the better of him."

"Maybe." And there could be a place inside his heart where he cared for his son. Assuming he had a heart. I wouldn't name this, however, because it might give Jaus false hope.

"No need to bring me back for formal introductions," I said.

"For that, I'm grateful." Jaus turned onto the road leading toward his home, and the salty-briny smell of the sea swirled around us. Some might find it refreshing, but it only made me think of dresalods. I worried that after one of the upcoming attacks, Jaus wouldn't return home to me.

Jaus's footsteps slowed. "I was frightened for you, tiny mate."

"I remember you bathed me. Soothed me. And you held me."

He came to a stop, staring down at me with his jaws grinding together. "I wait to hold you forever, Rhoslyn. I fought death to keep you by my side."

I didn't think the ache in my heart could deepen, but it did.

"Was I that sick?" I croaked, overcome with heady emotion. He cared for me. Could caring deepen to love?

"The healers said you might not make it. You had a head injury, and the infection . . ." He growled. "I beat that back as well." His gaze met mine. "Know that I will fight anything to keep you by my side."

It hurt to breathe. I tried to swallow but it wouldn't go down.

"Jaus," I gulped out.

"Don't speak. You need to rest." He continued to his home and nodded to the guards, who watched until we were inside, pulling the door closed behind us.

Jaus took the stairs to the first level. In no time, he laid me on our bed. "Sleep, little one. I'll watch over you. I'll keep everything dangerous away."

I wanted to reach out to him, to hold him like he'd

done me, but I couldn't keep my eyelids open. Despite doing nothing other than ride in his arms, my leg throbbed. Drums pounded in my head, drowning out everything but their incessant rhythm.

Jaus gently covered me with a soft blanket. I swore he kissed my cheek. He murmured something soothing that made me want to slip away into sleep.

I swore he stood beside the bed, his mace clutched in his hand as if he'd challenge the world to protect me.

I must be wrong about the last because that would mean he . . .

Sleep rose up to claim me.

"Time for a bath, tiny mate," Jaus said three days later, bustling into the bedroom and walking over to stand beside where I lay.

I'd slowly healed. I could remain awake most of the day now, and my leg barely hurt any longer. He still wouldn't allow me to walk, stating the royal healer insisted I must rest for at least another week. I was heartily tired of resting.

"I'll change the bedding while you soak in the water," he said.

My skin tingled at the thought of how he'd bathed me before I was injured, of his hands roaming my body with a skill that made my heart sing and my soul weep.

Before I could say a thing, he scooped me up and

carried me down one level to the washroom. The tub steamed, and fragrant herbs floated on the surface along with what looked like flower petals.

"Will you bathe with me?" I boldly asked. He obviously cared for me. He'd wanted me before I was injured. Surely that hadn't changed.

His eyes slid away from mine. "I should take care of the bed."

"Alright." I kept my hurt inside and my voice light.

He sat me on the edge of the tub. "Can you remove your clothing yourself and sit in the water or do you need my help?'

I didn't want to force this. If he'd changed his mind and he no longer wanted me, pushing him to do things he didn't desire would only prolong my torture. Somewhere between flying on Feyla in his arms after the hunt and waking in the palace, I'd fallen in love with my mate. According to Jaus, it was to be expected, but that didn't make my feelings any less real.

"I can do it," I said in a small, hollow voice.

Frowning, he studied my face. "You're still in pain." He sighed. "I'll help you."

"No!" I lowered my voice. "No. I'm not in any pain at all." To prove my point, I hopped off the side of the tub, landing squarely on my bare feet. Slowly, I tested adding more weight to my leg, finding it only vaguely twinged at the pressure. "See?" Peering up at him through my lashes, I studied his stoic face.

He still wouldn't look at me, though his hand stretched toward me. He'd grab me if I started to fall.

Too bad I'd already fallen.

"You're doing well," he finally said.

"I'm all better." To prove it, I lifted the tunic I wore over my head and tossed it aside. I wore nothing beneath.

His breath caught, but other than the tightening of his jaw, he continued to stare at the wall beyond me. Perhaps I was mistaken, and he was thinking of me? Thinking of someone and loving them could have very different meanings. Which was it? If I didn't test this, I'd never find out. Better to make things clear than wallow in pain forever in feelings based on assumptions.

His hand remained stretched toward me. Did it tremble?

Turning carefully, I climbed the short flight of stairs and sat on the side of the tub, dropping my legs into the water. I gasped at the heat.

"You're in pain." He lifted me and gently lowered me into the water. I swore his fingers lingered on my thighs before he eased them away.

"I'm not hurting anywhere." Other than in my heart. "The water's warm. It feels wonderful." I settled back in the seat and peered around. "Cloth and soap?"

"Sorry, I forgot." He hurried over to the shelf near the sink and brought them back, placing them on the edge of the tub. Pivoting sharply, he grabbed my tunic and placed it in the sink. Then he bolted toward the stairs.

"Could you wash my back?" I asked, studiously avoiding looking his way. "I can't reach."

With a heavy sigh, he returned to the tub, and I swore he heated the water with his gaze alone. Swallowing deeply, he dipped the cloth into the water, partly wrung it out, and lathered it with the soap.

I leaned forward.

He ran the cloth quickly up and down my back. A soft groan escaped him, and his strokes slowed. His other hand braced me on my shoulder. He teased the fingers of that hand down the length of my arm, creating patterns that bounced off my heart and shot to my core.

My moan slipped out from between my clenched teeth.

His hand stilled. "Pain?"

"No. It's . . ." I could keep everything inside and watch him, hoping for a sign, or I could take a huge risk and speak. "I love your touch. Your gentleness. How you make my pulse sing."

"What are you saying, Rhoslyn?" he croaked.

I met his gaze, my lungs shuddering to a halt when I found unbridled longing there. Perhaps he was finding it as difficult as me to talk about feelings, especially after his father's rejection. When someone you loved rejected you, it was very hard to trust another.

"I want you, Jaus," I said. "However I can have you."

"Tiny mate." He closed his eyes tight and shuddered. "I cannot bear to do anything that might make you suffer."

"If you don't love me, I'll suffer forever."

His eyes opened, widening. "Rhoslyn?" he breathed.

"I guess this is where I should beg, right?" My smile bloomed. I was convinced he was just as shy about sharing his feelings as me.

"I don't want you to beg any longer."

My smile dropped to nothing along with my heart. "If that means you don't want me, please tell me."

"I crave you," he growled. "All I want is to please you."

"I'll take desire, but I want more than that."

His gaze locked on mine. "What do you want, Rhoslyn?"

"You. Your body, your heart, and your soul."

CHAPTER 30
JAUS

"They're already yours." My voice croaked, and I didn't care. All that mattered was hearing what Rhoslyn might say next.

I watched her, bracing for her rejection.

"Jaus." Her smile rose but wavered. "I love you."

My guttural groan rang out. "*Mate.*" I shred my clothing to get out of it and climbed into the tub, gently lifting Rhoslyn and placing her on my lap. Wrapping everything I was around her, I trembled from my feelings. "Lovely mate. Precious mate. Mate who I love and adore above all others."

"Jaus." Her smile sunk into me, making my heart flip over. "You love me too?"

I nodded. Then, because I didn't want her to ever doubt me again, I spoke. "I love you. Adore you. I'll be on my knees forever solely to please you."

"You please me so much already. There's no need to

get down onto your knees." She shifted and wrapped her legs around me, her hands splayed wide on my chest. "What are we going to do about this love?"

"We're not going to beg."

She sent me a mischievous smile. "If you touch me, I might beg anyway. Is that alright with you?"

I couldn't believe this. "I suffered these past days, fear and worry for you consuming my every thought."

Her head cocked to the side. "Did you sleep on the floor beside the bed?"

"I couldn't risk lying beside you and inadvertently hurting you during the night. So yes, I laid on the floor. I tried to sleep, but it was fretful, nightmares of losing you drowned me. I didn't leave you other than to obtain food or bathe."

"You should've slept with me."

"I didn't dare risk bumping your leg. You were lying so still. I could barely see you breathe."

"I'm well now. All better." An impish grin filled her face. "I want you to treat me as your treasured mate."

"I will," I vowed.

"Then love me. Completely. I love your touch, but you need to know that I'm greedy. I'm going to stake my claim on you, mate."

My low laugh rang out. "I plan to do some staking myself."

"Then you'd better get started."

I cupped her precious face and stared into her eyes,

unable to believe she was well, let alone that she loved me. Her emotions shone in her eyes.

The female I thought I'd mate with eventually died. My father rejected me over and over. None of that mattered as long as I held my glorious Rhoslyn in my arms.

With that realization, the weight of the past I'd shouldered for too long slipped away.

I'd never lift that burden again.

I kissed her, gently cupping the nape of her neck, and when her lips parted with a moan, I unleashed the love glowing inside me, giving it to her in my kiss. The stroke of my hands down her shoulders and arms. And in the way I pulled her flush against my body.

My cock was on fire. I'd denied it—and us—for too long.

Deeping our kiss, I slid my tongue into her mouth. She whimpered and clung to my arms, pressing her breasts into my chest.

I wanted to love all of her, to be worthy of the love she so freely gave me. The thought that I could ruin this made me shake.

Then I realized she loved me despite how grumpy and gruff I was too much of the time. I'd denied her— denied us. I'd turned my back on my clan and the fates, refusing to accept my life could be better if I shared it with another.

Rhoslyn would give herself to me sweetly and with

complete trust. If she believed in me, how could I do anything less?

With a growl, I kissed her harder, my hands roving her body as a fever took hold inside me.

She stroked my chest and abs, teasing my nipples. Fire blazed through me, a flame only giving my body to her completely could extinguish.

Her head tipped back, and she moaned, rocking against my stiff cock. I'd never seen anyone as beautiful as my mate lost in the throes of passion.

I teased my fingertips up and down her sides, slowly moving closer to her core. When I reached her clit and rubbed it between my finger and thumb, her sharp cry rang out.

Clutching my arms, she stared into my eyes while I stroked her hard bud. I slipped a finger inside her, and she rode it, jerking up and down to impale herself on my hand.

When her inner walls started tightening, and her cries grew louder, she eased back away from me.

"Cock, Jaus. Give me your cock right now."

"My sole purpose in this world is to please you, tiny mate. Take my cock. Take all of me. I'm yours forever."

She rose up and grabbed my shaft, stroking it while I groaned and bucked up into her tight grip.

Then she centered it at her opening and dropped down.

CHAPTER 31
RHOSLYN

He was big and thick, and I couldn't wait to feel him impale me. My past experience was nothing compared to this moment.

Love made everything different. It was a brimming well, a gentle stream trickling over smooth rocks.

A raging inferno.

I lifted and plunged down again, using my weight to try to drive him deeper. Whimpering, I kept at it, though I wasn't making much progress.

With a low chuckle that turned me inside out, he latched onto my hips and when I dropped down again, he pushed while driving his cock up to meet me.

"Yes," I cried when he was fully seated. The rich burn sparked through me, only making me crave him more. "Claim me, Jaus, because I'm going to claim you."

His pendant flared, nearly blinding me with its

glorious light. I took it as a sign of approval. It picked me for him, and I should've trusted the spirits of the Azuris Clan from the start.

Gazing into each other's eyes, we rocked together, the water sloshing around us.

"Mate. Precious mate." His hand slid between us, and he pressed something down. It stroked across my clit until it latched on and hummed.

"What . . .?"

"My spur, love." He sent me a cocky grin. "Do you like it?"

It was all I could do to breathe or think. Latched onto my bud, the spur sucked, sending shockwaves through me.

Jaus lifted me up and pushed me back down. He thrust his hips to meet me each time, driving himself deep within me. Through it all, his spur loved my clit, sucking and tugging until I was splintering into so many pieces, I'd never find myself again.

It was too soon. Too much. I wasn't sure I could take it.

But when he started moving faster, spiking his cock up inside me, I was with him, drawing in what he had to give and whimpering that I needed more.

I was a tempest, a furious storm at sea, roaring toward the shore. There was no stopping me, and I let it lift me and sweep me along with it.

I came all at once, shuddering in his arms. He milked

it out of me, thrusting deeply, driving me to the edge and down the other side once more.

With a groan, he joined me, holding me tight.

Shuddering.

Keeping me safe like he'd done from the moment I met him.

CHAPTER 32
JAUS

"Your Azuris pendant isn't glowing any longer," Rhoslyn said. She lifted it. Stroked it. "Will it light up again?"

I shook my head. "It served its purpose. Our hearts are woven together. Our bond is complete."

"Ah." Leaning close, she kissed my chest. "I'm glad your clan gave you to me."

"And you to me. You, Rhoslyn, are perfect," I growled in her ear. "You were supposed to only bathe. You still need rest."

"You were supposed to only wash my back."

"I have no regrets." Wait. "You don't either . . . do you?"

"Not one bit." She smiled up at me with the open cheerfulness she'd shown already. Had she started falling in love with me from the start like I had with her?

I cleared my throat and spoke the words embedded

in my heart. "I feel as if the stars have conspired to paint your image into existence—a masterpiece of ethereal beauty that captivated me from the moment I met you."

"Jaus." Her fingers tightened on my arms, and tears sparkled in her eyes. "That's beautiful."

Her shimmering hazel eyes danced like flickering flames—so full of life, bewitching me in a spell I had no wish to escape from. An ocean of emotions swirled in their depths, pulling at me much like the tides caused by the moon on the sea.

"I'll love you forever, tiny mate," I said softly.

"And I'll love you."

She moved and winced, though I sensed she masked most of her reaction.

"You've overdone it." I lifted her off my cock, which missed her tight warmth already. "Allow me to bathe you. I should've offered from the start." I placed her gently on the seat beside me and grabbed the cloth, lathering it in the fragrant soap. "You must remain still. Don't move or jar your leg."

"It barely hurts."

"You should not have ridden me."

"Regrets?" she teased.

"Never," I growled. "But you're going to rest and continue to heal. I'll minister to you, doing everything that you need. Like this." I gently washed her face, taking the cloth down her neck and around to her nape. After rinsing off the lather, I tugged her off the seat and laid her across my lap.

"More?" she asked, her eyelids half-shuttered and her voice smoky and husky. "I'm ready."

My cock rose, but it would have to wait. It should be sated for now. It smacked against my abs, insisting it wasn't.

"I'm going to treat you gently, my tiny mate," I snarled.

She pouted, not put out by my grumbling for even a second. "What if I need you to help me heal?" Her fingers encircled my cock, stroking it.

My groan ripped through me.

What a challenge my mate threw out. How could I not rise to the occasion?

"I. Will. Bathe. You!"

Her saucy grin rose. "Alright. I'll behave and allow you to . . . *bathe* me."

She settled on my lap while I carefully washed her hair. And when I placed her back on the seat and started running the cloth across her chest, she clung to my arms. Her head tilted back, her lips parted, and she thrust her breasts into my hand.

"See?" she said in a husky voice. "I'm behaving."

I was being driven out of my mind. I wanted her again, and despite telling myself I needed to wait or I could injure her, I kept falling into her gaze and the need flaring there.

I washed her arms and belly, then spread her legs.

A smile teased across her lips as I ran the cloth over her thighs, taking care where she was wounded. When I dragged the scrap of fabric between her legs, she bucked up against my hand, moaning.

"Still behaving," she barked. "Not doing anything to make you eager to fuck me."

My cock was stiffer than my mace. It ached, and nothing was going to take away this pain other than claiming her once more.

Stepping out of the tub, I grabbed a drying cloth from the cupboard. I lifted Rhoslyn out of the water and ran the cloth all over her, making sure I pressed down on her clit while carefully drying between her legs.

She clung to my shoulders, her knees shaking, and when I looked up from where I knelt in front of her, she sent me a sultry smile.

Sweeping her up in my arms, I carried her up the stairs to our bed and laid her on the surface.

I could change the sheets later.

Much later.

Rising over her, I braced myself while I kissed her. Then I trailed my lips down her neck to her breasts and sucked a nipple into my mouth.

When I traced my fingers between her legs, I found her wet for me already. The fates and my clan had truly gifted me with an amazing woman.

She shifted her hips up to meet my fingers, and her heady moan made my cock spike against my belly.

While I sucked on her nipple, I continued to rub her clit. She whimpered and thrust herself against me, her fingers weaving through my hair and finally grasping my horns.

Unable to resist any longer, I spread her legs wider and pushed inside her.

We both groaned.

I moved slowly, carefully, not wishing to jar her leg but unable to resist getting caught up in the wonder of being with her completely.

She wrapped her legs around me and pushed her heels against my ass as I moved within her, driving my cock deeper.

"Jaus," she cried. "Jaus . . ."

Her head thrashed on the pillow while I continued rocking against her, still taking care so as not to hurt her.

"Please," she said.

Her body tightened around me, her tight sheath milking my cock sweetly.

When she came, I joined her, pumping within her until her shudders slowed. I eased to her side, taking her with me, keeping us locked together.

"I'll remain here all day, love," I whispered. "I'll hold you. Protect you. And give you a soft pillow on my chest."

"Muscular pillow, and I love it," she mumbled against my skin. "Rest a second, but don't fall asleep, because I'm going to ride you again soon."

CHAPTER 33
RHOSLYN

"Wake, tiny mate," Jaus called out cheerfully.

I slanted my eyelids to where he stood near the bed. Sunlight streamed through the windows behind him.

"You've slumbered long enough," he said. "I've finished my work, and the rest of my day belongs to us."

Could there be anything better than spending time with him? We'd loved each other all night long and well into the morning. Only when he'd completely worn me out had I fallen asleep in his arms.

I sat up, the covers falling off my naked body. "What would you like to do today?"

His gaze smoldered as he took in my frame. All I could think about was his mouth on mine, his hands roaming everywhere, and the weight of him settling on top of me. My belly fluttered, and my mouth went dry.

"You tempt me, tiny mate." He shook his head, his hair shifting across his shoulders. "But I have plans for you today that include more than driving myself deep into your body."

"What could be better than that?" I quipped, shifting the rest of the covers aside and sliding off the bed. I was pleased that my leg barely hurt when I rounded the bed and strode up to him.

"Rhoslyn," he growled. "You should not be walking on your leg."

"It's better. I'm better."

"I nearly lost you."

"We face death too often. It makes me want to savor the time we still have."

"You're right." He swept me up in his arms and took me back to the bed, laying me on the surface. "We shouldn't waste a single moment." He kissed me with desperation, like I was the link to everything he'd ever sought. His touch was as delicious as always.

It pushed aside everything in my mind but the feel of being with him.

AFTER WE BATHED, dressed, and ate a hearty meal, Jaus grabbed a pack he'd left on the kitchen counter and tossed it over his shoulder.

With his mace on his back, he took me to the balcony and called Feyla. She swooped down like a spear spiraling toward my chest and landed with a heavy thud on the stone surface. He hooked his bag on her lowest neck spike and strode over to stand in front of her.

I hovered near the wall, my breathing shallow. How could I not be intimidated by this majestic beast?

She dipped her head forward, snorting as she sniffed him, and he held her face, kissing her brow. When she nudged him playfully, he laughed and held steady.

"Come closer, tiny mate." He held his hand out to me. "Truly, she won't harm you."

"She's big."

His low chuckle rang out. "As am I, but you've tamed me."

"Have I?"

"Haven't you noticed that I cannot stay away from you?"

I had, and each time he sought me out, I fell further in love with him.

"Truly, I am the roll you named me," he added with a laugh.

While I was still uncertain about Feyla, I trusted Jaus implicitly. I took his hand, and he tugged me over to stand with my back pressed against his chest, his arms around me.

Feyla delicately sniffed me, and when she chuffed, my laugh burst out.

"See? She loves you as much as me," he said.

I wasn't sure about that, but my amazement pushed

aside my fear, and I tentatively touched her face. "Her scales are softer than I thought they'd be."

She seemed to nod.

My eyes widened. "Does she understand what I say?"

"Perhaps. No one knows. But a vox's perception can be uncanny at times. I owe my life to her. She's protected me more times than I can count."

Because I was grateful for that, I also kissed her brow.

She huffed and nudged my belly, though gently, and I stroked the side of her face.

"She adores you just like I do, mate." Jaus took my hand and led me around to her side, where he lifted me onto her spine. He leaped up behind me, his arms wrapping around my waist. "We ride."

A tap of his heels, and Feyla sprang into the air, her wings snapping out and flapping.

He guided her above the city, aiming for the enormous mountains in the distance towering all the way to the clouds.

Warm sunlight kissed my skin, and the flap of Feyla's wings soothed me. There was something wonderful about flying, and I could see why his people bonded with voxes.

I snuggled back against him, savoring his warmth. "Where are we going?"

"To my estate in the foothills of the mountains."

"I thought you only owned your home by the sea," I said.

"My mother raised me at the estate, but once I moved to the city, I rarely returned." His voice hollowed out. "It's been hard to go there since she died."

"I'm sorry. Tell me about her?"

"She was kind. Sweet. She loved to prepare my favorite meals, and she made me work with her in the gardens."

"I'm trying to picture you, my burly orc warrior, pulling weeds and digging in the dirt." The thought made me smile.

"I was more apt to fling the dirt around than dig in it as she told me."

"I bet you were a sweet orcling."

"Whatever sweetness I possessed was driven from me during my military training."

"I don't believe that. You may have developed a hard shell on the outside, but you're still squishy inside, and I love that you are."

"Mate." He kissed my temple.

"Is that her bracelet on your bureau?"

"It is. She wore it all the time. It was a gift from *her* mother. I couldn't bear to throw it away. At first, I could barely look at it. Now, when I see it, it makes me smile."

"Time softens the sadness and makes it easier to remember the good."

"You're right."

We left the city and traveled over open fields where I saw orcs managing crops and small houses also with metal exteriors.

"The dresalods come this far from the sea?"

"They advance until we kill them all," he said grimly. "Even as far as my mother's estate once."

"There's no place safe from them, then, is there?"

"They haven't yet traveled past the mountains. My brother's determined to eliminate the threat permanently, though I don't know how he'll do it. They breed fast and don't appear to care if they die. They used to only come at night, but lately, they've become bolder. They attack much more often and now challenge the sun."

"Where do you put the dead bodies?" I hadn't seen any when we walked through the city or lying on the shore after the most recent battle, not for long, that is.

"We take them out on a peninsula and dump them back into the sea. Their fellow dresalods eat them."

"Maybe bury the bodies so they have less to eat."

"We've thought of that, but at least fifty attack each time and few are driven back into the sea. That's too many to bury every few months."

Or every week if they kept coming more often.

The situation was untenable. There had to be a way to end this. "Would you consider moving far from the sea, where the dresalods won't reach?"

"The Azuris Clan's home is in the city. We'll remain there until the day we die."

I couldn't bear to lose him or anyone else living around us.

Under his guidance, Feyla flew lower, coasting

toward a two-story silver home sitting like a jewel in the middle of a large field. She landed in the front next to a pretty garden, and we slid off her back.

Jaus laid his pack on the ground nearby.

"I hire gardeners now," Jaus said as Feyla took off, soaring toward the enormous mountain range beyond the house. "No more digging in the dirt or pulling weeds for me." His eyes scanned the building. "I don't keep regular staff inside. A few come monthly to keep the place tidy and drive away vermin."

"All these years, you've held onto it, yet you don't live here?"

"Someday, maybe."

"I can understand why you might not want to. My parents didn't have a home to leave me and Lyneth. If they had, the memories might've haunted us." Although, they might've also given us comfort. "I took my mother's mortar and pestle, plus her gathering baskets with me when we moved into a small place we rented. I enjoyed using her things."

"I'm glad you and your sister had each other." Lifting his pack, he took my hand.

"What's on the agenda for today?" I asked as he led me around the side of the building.

"I thought we could have a picnic like I used to long ago with my mother. Replace some of my sad memories with good ones."

CHAPTER 34

JAUS

"Fifteen years ago, I helped my mother plant these flowering trees," I said as I led my mate among them. "They're so tall now. Back then, they were no taller than me."

"They're beautiful." Rhoslyn paused and pulled down a branch, sniffing the pale purple blossoms. "They smell amazing."

"My mother loved the perfume. She told me once she wanted to smell it every day of her life. I transplanted one of the trees to a spot near her grave on the outskirts of the city. Now she's surrounded by the perfume each summer."

"That's wonderful. We . . . didn't find much of my parents to bury. My sister will visit their grave." Her sigh of sadness bled out. "I won't be able to see it again."

"I'm sorry." I hugged her, and we continued walking.

In the center of the grove, my mother had left a small

area bare, planting it only with sweetgrass. Two stone benches flanked the sides. I waved to them. "When the flowers bloomed, my mother would sit here and close her eyes, sucking in the scent."

"It's a lovely spot."

"You're the only one I've ever wanted to share it with."

She leaned into my side, and I sucked in the sympathy she so willingly gave.

I spread a blanket in the center of the open area, and we sat.

Rhoslyn leaned back on her palms with her legs outstretched. Her eyelids slid closed, and she lifted her nose. "I love it here already. It smells wonderful."

"I thought it might make me sad to come here again. I haven't returned to this grove since she was killed by the shaydes."

"I wish I could say something to help ease your pain."

"I feel the same for you."

We linked our fingers together.

"Just being here with you makes a difference. I feel . . . happy," I said. It wasn't hard to smile, and as my smile grew, some of the rough edges on my sadness smoothed.

"Your mother would be proud of all you've accomplished. I bet she loved you a lot."

"She did." I'd never doubted that. My father rejected me, but she'd done all she could to make up for his lack, and it was enough. "I just realized I don't need him."

"Your father."

I nodded. "All these years, I mourned that he didn't want me. But my mother made my life special, and you, my tiny mate, make me feel complete." Finally, I felt free of the pressure to do something—anything—that might please him. "I spent too much time hoping he'd see I was worthy and accept me. All this time, it didn't really matter. I don't need him."

"I think it's natural for a child to want both their parents to love them."

"It was harder to distance myself from him because he gives everything he has to Madr."

"I don't sense you're jealous of him."

I shook my head. "I love my brother. He's amazing. He's two years younger and we trained together with the palace staff, something my father asked of my mother. He planted flowers on her grave with his own hands, not asking staff to do it for him."

"He's nothing like your father."

"Not one bit."

She laid back on the blanket, watching the clouds drift by overhead. Since I didn't want to spend our precious time here mourning, I pushed aside everything but the thought of how amazing my mate was, how much I ached to make her happy.

Picking a strand of grass, I tickled the bushy end across her face, tracing it down her nose to her chin.

She laughed, her bright eyes meeting mine. "What are you up to, mate?'

"Would you like me to glide this bit of grass across all of your body?"

Her breath caught. "I can't imagine anything better than that."

"Oh, I believe I can show you something better."

I peeled off her clothing and mine and traced the soft grass down between her breasts. Around each nipple that budded so perfectly.

A moan tumbled from her lips. "I shouldn't be aroused by something so simple. But I bet you could touch me with anything, and I'd fall apart."

I replaced the grass with my hands, teasing her nipples while my cock throbbed with need. Stroking down across her belly, I parted her thighs and crawled between them. She was slick just for me.

When I licked her, her moan ripped out once more. She clutched my horns and shifted her hips up.

"You're lighting me on fire, mate," she said.

I was too busy sucking on her clit to respond. She tasted sweet. Like life and our love.

I slid a finger inside her, growling with eagerness since she was so wet. Her back bowed, and she stroked my horns desperately. Her gasps of joy echoed around us.

Lifting her up onto her hands and knees, I curled my body around hers. "Does this hurt your leg?"

"I can't feel anything but an overwhelming need for you, Jaus. Please. Don't wait."

I took her with one thrust, burying myself to the hilt

inside her. Bracing her hips, I pulled out and drove myself back inside.

"Your body sucks on my cock so beautifully," I growled.

"Faster, Jaus. Please."

I reached around and tugged on her clit, rolling it, and she pushed back hard to each of my thrusts. Our moans filled the meadow, chasing away any lingering ghosts, and the heady perfume of the trees filled my senses.

There was nothing better than loving my mate.

Raw hunger filled me, and I moved faster, driven on by her cries of pleasure.

When she shuddered, her spine arching, I shouted and joined her in bliss.

CHAPTER 35
RHOSLYN

After napping, we dressed and ate the meal he'd brought, lounging on the blanket.

I fed him a succire, a sweet berry that ripened this time of year, and he fed me so many, I couldn't take another bite. Soon, our lips were coated with redness, and we were kissing, tasting the fruit on each other's tongues.

Lying on the blanket, we held hands.

"Would you like a tour of the house?" he asked.

"I'd love one." Rising, I looked down at him. He was so handsome, so perfect. It made my heart ache. I feared something this wonderful would be stolen from me just like my parents were and then my life in the village. I couldn't bear to lose him.

"Sad, my love?" Sitting up, he tugged me down onto his lap and held me, curling forward to rest his chin on the top of my head.

The last thing I wanted to do was hand him my sorrow-filled thoughts when his own appeared to have fled. "I'm never sad when I'm with you."

"Tiny mate," he grumbled. "You say things that are much too sweet for a gnarly orc commander like me."

Looking up at him, I stroked his dear face. "You deserve sunshine and peace every day of your life. All the best life has to offer."

"That's you, Rhoslyn. You." He rose with me in his arms and placed me on my feet. "Let me show you where I grew up. Then we'll have to fly home if we hope to reach it before dark."

At my nod, we gathered everything and strode toward the path weaving among the trees. I glanced back one last time, savoring the sweet smell of the flowers and the serenity of the meadow. "Let's come here again."

He squeezed my hand. "Yes, soon."

We entered the building from the back, walking through a kitchen, the attached dining room, and across a foyer on the front. Stairs went up to the second level, but Jaus led me through two sitting areas first, pausing in the second.

"My mother and I would play games here or read in the evening." He gestured to the big full bookcase.

I trailed my fingers across the spines. "So many."

"My mother loved reading. She enjoyed romances, and she'd read them to me, skipping the good parts with a blush on her face."

I laughed. "I doubt you wanted your mother to read them aloud to you."

"You're right." He tugged me backward into his arms and held me, and his happiness sunk into my bones. "Her love of romance was passed on to me, however."

"You still read romances? I can't quite believe that. I picture you reading long treatises about battles and strategies to win a war."

"I read those for work, but when I have free time, there isn't much better than escaping into a world where love conquers all."

"The grumpy orc I met in the forest didn't act like a male who enjoys romance." Although, only now did I remember the books that looked like romances in his home that I dismissed as military-related with odd titles.

"I may not have acted romantic, but the actions and words I read over the past years sunk in. Haven't I been romantic with you since you came to the city?"

In some ways, perhaps as much as he could.

"I believe I am the roll inside you once named me, for you at least," he said.

I turned in his arms and kissed him, melting against his battle-hardened frame.

"You distract me in a delicious way," he said when we pulled apart. "Come. I'll show you the room I slept in when I was an orcling."

We took the stairs to the second level.

He gestured to the first doors we passed in the hall. "Guest rooms." We walked by another he didn't name before stopping at the one at the end. "This was mine." He swung the panel open and urged me inside.

I took in the bureaus and the span of windows along one side. Pictures of various creatures hung on the walls, and a box overflowing with toys had been placed in a corner.

He crossed the room and looked out the windows while I puttered around, touching everything because each had meant the world to him.

Sunlight streamed around him when he turned away from the windows, striding over to stand with me beside a painting I suspected must be of his mother. The resemblance was uncanny. He'd gotten his hair and eyes from her, his height and the breadth of his shoulders from his father.

"She was lovely," he whispered.

"Beautiful. You're lucky to have this house, your things still waiting for you to pick them up again. All these memories here to delve into when you're ready."

"I'm sorry you weren't able to remain in your parent's home back at the village."

"Without their income, I couldn't afford to stay. We moved into a smaller home and made new memories there."

"Now we share a home together in the city."

"We'll fill it with love." And orclings if the fates blessed us.

"We should go," he said, his gaze lingering on each item in the room.

His big bed was covered with a blanket made up of patches.

He stroked it. "My mother made this. I left it here because it was one more reminder of my loss."

"Would you like to take it with you now? We could put it on our bed at home."

He nodded and gave me a sweet kiss. "I would. Thank you mate."

"For what?"

"For loving me."

CHAPTER 36
JAUS

We flew home on Feyla, and when she landed on the balcony, I lifted Rhoslyn off the vox's spine and placed her on the stone surface.

She hurried over to stand in front of Feyla. "Thank you for the ride. And thank you for being here for Jaus." Leaning forward, she kissed Feyla's forehead.

My vox nudged Rhoslyn, huffing. Nothing made me happier than seeing the two females I loved adoring each other.

As I took Rhoslyn's hand and we walked toward the door, Feyla lifted off. She swooped around above my house, chirping, before her shrill cry rang out.

It was echoed by the shrieks of dresalods scrambling out of the sea.

My heart froze.

"You said they wouldn't come back for a few

months," Rhoslyn whispered, her wide-eyed gaze shooting around. Shakes took over her body. She must be remembering when one nearly killed her.

The scrape of claws rang out. They'd reached the wall already.

I bellowed for Feyla and pulled my mace.

"Inside, mate," I said hoarsely, handing her the bag I'd used to carry our food. "Bar the door and don't open it. Please stay inside where you're safe."

She clung to my tunic. "Stay with me." Color filled her face. "I'm sorry. I didn't mean that. I know you have to leave. The city needs you. But . . ."

"I understand. I can't bear to lose you either." I kissed her fast, wishing we had more time. With each battle, the odds I wouldn't return home to her rose. "I'll come back to you, tiny mate. This I promise."

Her eyes glistened with tears, and her mouth was a hard slash across her face, but she nodded.

"I love you," was all she said as she left me, opening the door. She turned back to face me. "I'll watch you leave, and then I'll go inside."

Feyla landed behind me on the deck.

Dropping my mace, I rushed to Rhoslyn and lifted her up, slanting my mouth across hers.

She wrapped her arms around my shoulders, clinging.

"Go," she said when I lifted my head. "I'll be all right. Take care of yourself and don't worry about me."

She slipped from my arms and entered the building.

I waited until the bar banged into place before spinning and with my mace in hand, leaping onto Feyla's spine. She took flight, soaring toward the ocean in a wild flurry.

At least a hundred dresalods floundered through the waves, rushing toward the shore. Others clambered up the smooth walls while those on the top shot flaming arrows down upon them. Some of the creatures fell while others climbed over them.

One of these days, we wouldn't defeat them all. They'd overrun us, and it would be over.

Never, my heart cried. I'd battle each and every one of them to protect my mate and my people. Every person living in the city felt the same.

I guided Feyla down toward the shore, and as she flew just above a legion of dresalods, I slammed my mace through them, hitting one and then another. Before they could latch onto me with their claws, Feyla spiraled upward, taking me to safety.

She made one pass after another until my arm ached and my legs were covered with gashes from the beasts' claws.

"More," I cried, struggling to find strength within me to keep fighting. I'd never give up, never allow them past the wall.

A few scrambled up onto the top where orcs shouted battle cries and attacked. They drove them off, the creatures falling many stories to the bloody sand below. The carcasses piled up, and it was going to take days to remove them all.

I guided Feyla down for another pass, grateful to see no more dresalods leaving the sea.

How many times could we keep battling until there were none of us left? I didn't want to think about that. All that mattered was killing one and then another.

As Feyla swept above the back of the last legion, I smacked my mace into as many as I could.

Something raked down my spine, and I cried out with pain.

I was dragged off Feyla.

I fell, landing hard in the sand.

CHAPTER 37

RHOSLYN

How could I do anything but pace while Jaus and our entire city was in danger? It didn't take much for the memory of the dresalod attack in the street to tell me what our brave warriors faced.

"There has to be a way to keep them from attacking." Back in the fortress, we'd traded two women a year for the orc's protection from the shaydes. It appeared the orcs protected everyone, even themselves. But this situation wasn't sustainable. The dresalods reproduced too rapidly for us to kill them all. Eventually, they'd wear down our numbers and . . . I didn't want to think of what might happen then.

The solution lay in driving them into the sea and making sure they never returned. But how?

I made the bed, cringing each time someone cried out from the sea side of the city. The whoosh of mounted voxes flying overhead drew my eye, and I watched them pass, rushing to the window where I clutched the sill while the mounted beasts flew down toward the shore.

A dresalod clambered up over the wall, where the guards attacked it, killing it but losing one of their own. The orc bellowed and clutched his abdomen where he'd been impaled while his friends dragged him away from the dresalod carcass. Someone helped the orc rise and took him down the inner stairwell. Did healers wait for him at the bottom?

I should be there with them, tending the wounded. It would occupy my mind and I'd feel useful. I was no warrior, so taking up a mace and leading a charge would only put me in harm's way.

But healing . . . That was bred into my bones.

In the kitchen, I left a note for Jaus in case he returned before me. Then I gathered up the herbs he'd purchased for me, sighing at how few I had that could be used to treat wounds.

Lindenmint, of course. I crushed about half of what I had left and stirred it into boiling water, making a slurry much like the tea I drank each morning. Then I added more leaves until it formed a paste I could apply. I left it to cool and rushed up to our bedroom, where I found an old tunic full of holes and ripped it into strips for bandages.

Back downstairs, I rolled the bandages and tucked them into my basket, adding the few other herbs I'd used in the past to treat cuts and abrasions.

The basket was only one-quarter full; it felt like too little. I needed to return to Liall's shop and buy the other medicinal herbs I saw when we were there.

After thoroughly washing a few wooden spoons, I put them inside the basket. I'd use them to apply the lindenmint paste. I located a few small, covered jars and started scooping the pungent astringent into them.

My fingers stilled, and I stared forward, remembering.

The dresalod spied me hiding in the narrow nook between the buildings. It rushed toward me, smacking its claws against the silver walls.

I cringed, whimpering, trying to shrink into myself to escape what looked like my certain death. My breathing was ragged, and my pulse pounded like a thousand drums in my ear.

Jaus was fully focused on battling the other two dresalods and couldn't help me.

The dresalod reeled up and flung itself toward me, its claws scrambling across the silver, seeking me. Over and over, while I nearly bit through my tongue to keep from screaming. If I distracted Jaus for even a second, the dresalods he battled could hurt him.

He killed the second one just as the third struck true, its claw sinking all the way through my thigh. My guttural groan wrenched up my throat.

The beast yanked its claw free and stabbed toward me again, this time aiming for my heart. When I was dead, it could pluck me from the nook and eat me at its leisure.

I had too much to live for.

Jaus . . .

With a battle cry burning up my throat, I flung my cup of tea at the dresalod.

Shrieking, it spiraled, its front claws snapping at the air.

Where the lindenmint tea hit, its exoskeleton steamed and rippled as if it was being eaten by something highly corrosive. It collapsed on the ground, writhing.

Jaus grabbed me and pulled me out of the nook, placing me behind him.

The dresalod flipped over and sprung to its feet, spinning in a circle while its body continued to steam.

Shrieking like the dresalods did right now outside our city walls, the one in my memory rose and hobbled down the street. Jaus gave chase, his bloody mace lifted.

I collapsed on the ground and didn't wake until days later in the palace, but I assume Jaus slayed the final beast.

But it had steamed . . .

"Did the tea cause a reaction?" I whispered, clutching the glass jar so tightly, I worried I'd crush it. "It's not possible. A simple tea couldn't harm a dresalod's exoskeleton, could it?" Staring down at the poultice I'd made; I ran over the scene in my mind once more. "Maybe it was the hot water."

But my mind kept returning to the lindenmint.

"There's no harm in trying."

I rushed to the kitchen and put a big pot of water on to boil, adding the rest of the lindenmint. I hated to think I could interfere with the battle with potentially useless tea, but if I ran this test, I could confirm or shoot down my theory. I just needed to make sure the brew was strong.

When it churned into a rolling boil, I simmered the tea, the minty-tangy scent filling the air and reminding me of when I was little, and my mother made us drinks we shared together. My childhood and teen years were filled with her smiles, my dad ruffling my hair, and the four of us sitting out front in the evening, staring at the stars with mugs of yummy tea in our hands.

If only something so wonderful could help my new people now.

When I felt like the water had sucked all the goodness from the tea's leaves, I left them there rather than strain them out. Might as well go all in with this experiment. I found a cover and sealed the top of the pan.

Then, with a too-big pair of Jaus's leather gloves protecting my hands, I carefully carried the pan down the back stairs and out onto the street.

Pandemonium greeted me, weapon-carrying orcs rushing in all directions in an attempt to protect the city.

Where was a dresalod when I needed one? Not that I'd invite one within the city walls to test my brew. Where could I do it, however?

Ah, the wall. I'd seen them carrying the injured orc down a set of stairs. If I could reach the top and avoid being injured again myself, I could dump the slurry over the side and watch. If it worked, I'd see it almost immediately, and if it didn't, at least I'd be relatively safe on the top of the wall.

I wove among orcs rushing in one direction or another, keeping close to the buildings as I made my way to the wall. The staircase was clear, and I crept up it to the top, trying not to slosh the liquid all over myself. I'd be scalded if I did.

There would be no way of knowing if the boiling water caused the damage I believed I saw or the herb, but at least I'd soon know if hot lindenmint tea caused a reaction.

This could be an invaluable weapon for my people.

My people. I shook my head at the thought. They were mine, however, the entire city. And once things had stabilized again, I was going to see how my healer skills could be used to help others.

For now, I'd donned the cloak of a warrior with tea as my weapon.

Shouts and cries greeted me at the top, though at least no dresalods scurried across the smooth surface.

I lugged the pan over to the edge and peered down. A dresalod was scrambling up the wall directly beneath me. It would be the perfect test subject.

I flung the lid aside, and it clattered on the stone

floor. Then I hefted the pan and dumped it directly on the dresalod.

Bellows rang out behind me, and fully armed warriors rushed my way.

"Get back," one cried.

Another growled. "What are you doing here, foolish female?"

And the worst of all. "Grab her. Arrest her!"

Arrest me for what?

The pan fell from my hands, clattering on the stone floor. As numerous orcs stomped toward me, I peered over the wall. The dresalod had fallen to the ground. It writhed, and its body was steaming. Then it went still as the brew completely dissolved its exoskeleton, leaving only a pile of mush and twitching spiked limbs behind.

A cry from over the sea drew my eye. I knew that voice, plus the shriek of that vox.

Feyla spiraled toward the sand, Jaus on her back. A dresalod leaped toward her, landing behind Jaus. She twisted and roared, swooping back upward.

Jaus wasn't with her.

As the orcs on the wall grabbed my arms and dragged me away, I screamed for Jaus.

I spied him lying on the sand.

He wasn't moving.

CHAPTER 38
JAUS

When I hit the ground, the wind was knocked from my lungs. While I floundered, struggling to suck in air, I heard my precious mate shouting my name. I couldn't breathe, but my eyes worked fine.

Orc warriors dragged her away from the wall shouting something inane that sounded like they were arresting her.

Absolutely not.

A growl built inside me, and when it burst free, I leaped to my feet—just in time to swing my mace out at an attacking dresalod. I drove spikes halfway through its skull.

It flopped on the sand, and I peered around.

The rout was over; the remaining dresalods rushed back into the sea, leaving the carcasses of their brethren behind.

One steamed near the wall, but I dismissed it. They'd taken my mate, and I was going to blast through them to rescue her.

Tightening my grip on my mace, I stomped toward the city. Feyla landed in the sand in front of me.

"Where were you?" I snarled.

She huffed.

"I'm sorry." The last thing I wanted to do was take my fury out on such a sweet creature.

She huffed again and nudged my belly with her nose.

I jumped onto her back and urged her into flight. We flew up and over the wall, but I didn't see my mate anywhere behind it. Taking my vox higher, I studied that part of the city, finally spying a cluster of orcs carrying a slight person among them.

I landed Feyla in the street just in time to watch them take Rhoslyn inside the prisoner holding area. When I raced over to it and banged on the closed door, someone called out from inside. "What do you want?"

"It's Commander Kreedaull. Let me in. You just stole my mate." It was all I could do not to break the door down with my mace.

"We didn't steal anyone, and we're not letting anyone in, not even you, Commander."

We'd see about that.

Pivoting, I released Feyla to return to her nest and stomped through city and right up to the front door of the palace. As if this was a social visit, the guards rushed to the doors ahead of me and swept them open, bowing as I passed and slammed my way into the foyer.

My bellow rang out in the empty foyer.

"What in the world is going—" Madr emerged from a parlor dressed for battle, though his armor was still undented and clean. He held his flail aloft, and the vicious look in his eyes told me I'd no longer have a head if he didn't recognize me. "Brother." His hand dropped to his side, the mace on the end of the chain clunking when it impacted with the floor. "*Someone* has been trying to keep me from joining the battle."

"It's over," I said.

"Success?"

I shrugged. If we lost even one orc, I'd never call it a victory.

"What are you doing here?" Madr asked.

"The guards took Rhoslyn."

"What? Why?"

"I don't know. I left her at my home. At the end of the battle, I fell off Feyla—"

"You . . . fell off your vox?" He blinked for a moment. "How did that happen?"

I grumbled, stomping my feet. "I have no idea and it doesn't matter. My back hurts, but I doubt it's more than a scratch. Feyla's fine. I'm fine. I killed a bunch of dresalods and they're not fine. The rest returned to the sea."

"How does this involve Rhoslyn?"

"I saw her on the wall and heard the guards shouting they were going to arrest her. I followed on Feyla as they took her to the holding cells. They refused to allow me inside."

Madr scowled and lifted his arm.

"Yes, my prince?" one of the guards near the door cried, stepping forward.

"Take a contingent and go get my dear sister from the holding cells. Bring her here immediately. Be gentle; she's precious not only to me but my brother." Rage burnished his face. "And tell the warden he'd better have a good excuse as to why his underlings arrested her. Tell him I expect him to report here within the hour to share that reason."

"We'll leave immediately, my prince," the guard said, backing over to the others. After a quick conversation, one rushed from the foyer, down the hall, and the others took their stations at the door again. Within moments, I spied a group of guards racing past the window on the opposite side of the parlor, followed by a whoosh as their voxes took flight.

The warden would not refuse a direct order from the prince.

Agitated and ready to rip off some heads, I paced the foyer. Madr watched me with some amusement until I stopped in front of him and snarled.

His lips twitched before a somber look took over her face. "I'm sure she's fine. They won't harm her."

Because she was female, no one would touch even one hair of a precious being who might give us orclings. My mate meant much more to me than that, however, and I planned to tell her a thousand times a day once I held her in my arms again.

"Treating her decently is not enough for me," I stormed. "I'm going to follow them. She'll be frightened, worried about what's happening. I need to be there to reassure her."

"Stay here." Madr grabbed my arm, holding me back, and if I didn't love my brother dearly, I'd impale him with my mace. "By the time you reach the building, they'll be halfway back on their voxes."

Gripping his shoulder, I peered into his uncanny green eyes, so different from most orcs' dark gold. He'd inherited them from his mother. "I don't like this, Madr."

"I don't either. It'll be all I can do not to rip the warden apart when he humbly presents himself here." He guided me toward the parlor. "Come. Sit. Have a drink. She'll be here before you know it."

Gnashing my teeth, I followed him.

"You drove the dresalods away once more," he said, taking my mace and leaning it against a wall along with his flail.

"Always."

"My advisors are studying old texts and consulting with other kingdoms in the hope someone can help us arrive at a permanent solution."

He waved to a sofa, but I didn't sit. While he filled snifter glasses with a pale liquor, I paced in front of the fireplace, grumbling.

"Why are you here and not finishing off the battle?" the king asked from the doorway.

"It's over," I snarled, not in the mood to humor him today. "We killed as many as we could before the rest fled back into the sea." Because he was the king and my liege lord, even though I despised him, I gave him a short bow.

"Battling doesn't appear to have improved your mood," he said with a sniff, crossing the room to join Madr where he was finishing pouring beverages.

My brother left our father to serve himself and brought me a drink. I downed it in one gulp, placing the glass on a nearby table with a clang.

"More?" Madr asked.

"One's enough."

"It might cheer you up," the king said, turning with a drink in his hand. He watched me with speculation. "Why are you here?"

"Are you suggesting I'm not welcome?" I would no longer try to gain his praise or respect. If he was going to be nasty—which he always was—I might as well give it back as quickly as I received it. He deserved a taste of the way he'd treated me for my entire life.

He grunted and sipped his drink, watching me.

"My mate was on the wall during the battle," I told him. "I saw the guards take her, but when I followed with Feyla, I couldn't reach her before they took her inside the holding cells. They've refused to grant me access."

"Then why haven't you gone there?"

"I did. When they wouldn't release her, I came here for help." My anger fueled by fighting dropped away suddenly, and I sat again, bracing my elbows on my knees and my face in my palms. "My poor mate must be terrified, and I'm not there to hold her."

"Ask one of the guards to go get her," my father told Madr with a sigh.

"I already have. She should be here in no—"

The swoop of wings was followed by the scrape of claws on stone as a flight of voxes landed on the stone pad outside.

I roared to my feet and raced toward the foyer. "Rhoslyn. Rhoslyn!"

The front doors swept open, and my glorious, gorgeous mate strode inside, fury flushing her cheeks.

"I'll kill the warden and his minions," she snarled at the guards behind her. A whimper slipped from her lips. "Jaus fell. He could be dead, and I wasn't there to hold him!" Spying me standing in the entrance to the parlor, her eyes widened. "Jaus, you're alive. Jaus." As I rushed toward her, she staggered forward, collapsing into my arms.

I swept her up and kissed her, needing her reassurance as much as she needed mine. My tiny mate was here. She appeared unharmed, and everything was right in my world once more.

I pressed her against the wall and cupped her lush ass. Her legs wrapped around me, her heels tugging me flush against her frame. I devoured her mouth, giving into the craving that threatened to consume me whenever we touched. My tongue spiraled around hers, and—

"Hey, you two." Humor flooded Madr's voice. "Maybe save that for later?"

I lifted my head and studied her face. "You're not hurt? They didn't touch you or harm you, did they? I'll kill them regardless, but I need to know you're safe before I go rip that place apart."

"They actually treated me well. Other than when they hauled me away from the wall and through the city. They didn't lock me in a cell. In fact, when the palace guards arrived, they were offering me tea. But I don't care about that. I saw you fall, Jaus. You were hurt!" Her hands roamed my arms and torso, seeking wounds. "Where are you hurt, my love? I'll heal you."

"I'm uninjured. Only my pride was bruised when I slipped off Feyla. She appeared as shocked as me. I haven't fallen off her since the first time she allowed me to ride."

"You're sure you don't have any wounds?" Her eyes sparkled with tears.

I'd kill to reassure her. "I'm well. Grateful to hold you in my arms once more."

Her breath whooshed out. "I'm so happy." She burst into tears and sagged against me, sobbing into my chest.

I patted her back and carried her into the parlor, ignoring my father's huff. Sinking into a chair, I held her, murmuring soft words I hoped would comfort her. "I'm well, mate. Truly."

She looked up at me with tears streaking down her face. "Truly?"

"Absolutely."

"I'm grateful to hear the guards didn't harm you, sister," Madr said, sinking into a nearby chair. "Why were you at the top of the wall during a battle?"

"Oh!" Rhoslyn's gaze shot to my brother. "I must tell the king I've discovered a way to fight off the dresalods."

My father snorted and strode over to stand nearby. "*You've* discovered a way to defeat the dresalods? You're a puny human. Only worthy of bearing orclings to perpetuate our species."

"Father," Madr snarled, rushing to his feet. "Don't speak to her like that again."

Color flooded the king's face. "You, my son, do not tell *me* how to behave."

I eased my mate into the chair and stormed to my feet. With a snarl, I barreled into the king, taking us both to the floor. Landing hard on top of him, I drove the air from his lungs. I reeled back my fist, ready to drive it through his face, but Madr grabbed it, holding me back.

"He's not worth it," he hissed. "Stop, brother, before you do something we'll all regret."

Growling, I lifted myself off the king and went to my tiny mate, dropping to my knees in front of her and taking both of her hands in mine. "I love you, and I'm going to take you home."

"I want that more than anything, but I need to explain even if your . . . I won't even name him that. He doesn't deserve it." She shook her head, and her gaze sought Madr. "I'll share what I learned with you. You'll find a way to use this to our advantage." Her sneer fell on the king rising to his feet and straightening his clothing.

When he looked my way, he said nothing, and I swore fear flitted through his eyes. Good. He needed to learn how to hold his tongue and respect my strength even if he couldn't respect me as a person.

"While you were valiantly fighting off the dresalods." Rhoslyn's glare my father's way deepened. "I remembered what happened on the street when you fought off the ones who attacked us."

I tightened my fingers around hers. "I wasn't fast enough, and you paid the price."

"Up." She urged me to my feet. "I love having you kneeling in front of me, though we're wearing too much clothing—"

Madr coughed, and my love and my brother shared a grin.

I gathered her close and sat again with her nestled on my lap.

She leaned back against my chest, and only then did my anger with the king begin to fade. "I don't know if you recalled what I did before you killed the third dresalod. When it stabbed me, I acted on instinct. I had no weapon—"

"Here's one." Madr scooped a long blade off a mount on the wall and handed it to her.

"That was my father's," the king protested.

"And now it belongs to Rhoslyn." Death came through in Madr's voice, telling me the king had gone too far today for even my usually placid brother.

"Amazing." Rhoslyn studied the blade before looking up at me. "I'll need a sheath."

"It shall be yours."

"Is there a point to all this?" the king asked.

"Yes." My tiny mate nodded pertly. "I threw my very hot lindenmint tea at the dresalod. It smoldered, and I swear, before I passed out, I saw its exoskeleton melting."

Madr's breath caught. "Do you believe the hot liquid or the herb caused the reaction?"

She shrugged. "I'm not sure. When I remembered, I had to test it. I brewed a vat of lindenmint tea and dumped it over the wall, directly on a dresalod below."

"And?" The king leaned toward her. Even he was stunned by her words.

"I believe this could be a way to defeat them."

"I don't believe it. It's a coincidence," the king said with scorn. His sneer took me in. "We should've left her in the holding cell."

I wasn't going to point out again that when the king's guards arrived, I was about to have tea with the warden, not sit in a cell.

"I'm done here." Jaus rose with me in his arms. He shook his head at his father. "I don't need you. It took me some time to realize that, but now that I do, I finally feel free. All I need is my tiny mate, my Rhoslyn."

"And me," Madr chimed in.

"Always you, my brother." He smiled down at me. "Time to take you home."

He was safe. We were back together. Nothing else mattered.

"I believe I'm done as well," Madr said, grabbing his flail and Jaus's mace and following us to the foyer. "I don't suppose you have a place where I can sleep tonight?" He tucked Jaus's mace into the sheath on his back. I still carried the knife and took care not to slice Jaus or me with the wicked sharp blade.

"Where are you going, Madr?" the king cried, hurrying to the front door the guards so kindly opened. He continued out onto the walkway behind us.

"I disown you," Madr told him. He shot us a grin. "Damn, but it feels good to say that." He turned back to his father. "I've put up with your shit for too long, and like my brother, I will no longer do so. I don't care what you do with your crown. I don't care about you—not any longer." He patted Jaus's shoulder.

"You can sleep on our sofa," Jaus offered. "As soon as you'd like, you're welcome to fly out to my estate. You can remain there forever if you'd like."

"Ah, yes, I remember the property. I'll be happy to stay there until I can reopen my mother's home in the mountains and settle there."

"We can discuss it tonight," Jaus said. He whistled and a short time later, Feyla landed with a thud in the middle of a flowerbed. She frowned at the flowers, then took a big bite.

Jaus laughed, and Madr and I joined in.

The king continued to scowl.

"You can't go with them," he told Madr, and even I could hear the defeat in his voice. He'd driven both of his sons away. Was he finally realizing that if you were nasty to others, they eventually turned it back on you tenfold? Perhaps. I wasn't going to wait around to find out.

A leap, and Jaus landed on Feyla's back, still holding me in his arms. I turned to face him, snuggling close. I was exhausted, and I couldn't wait to get home.

"I'll be right behind you, flying on Brakkur," Madr called out. "And as for the dresalods, I've got a plan!"

CHAPTER 40

JAUS

"I need more lindenmint tea leaves," Rhoslyn insisted. "We need to stop for it on our way home."

"I just want to take you inside our house and hold you, mate. Tea can wait." Then it occurred to me what she was saying. I grinned at her and directed Feyla on a detour. "You're clever, mate. Very clever."

"There's nothing better than lindenmint tea, don't you think?"

I gave her a quick kiss as Feyla swooped lower and landed on the street not far from Liall's shop.

Many of our fellow orcs shopping in the big open plaza gave us odd looks, but Feyla wouldn't be the first vox to land somewhere other than on a balcony.

We left her to wait and hurried to Liall's herbal apothecary, where I let my mate chose. "Buy whatever you want, love."

She sent me a quick smile before nodding sharply. With a basket hanging over her arm and purpose, she rushed through the shop selecting one thing after another. We also bought all the lindenmint Liall had.

With our packages in a big sack, we flew to our home, Feyla landing beside Madr's vox, Brakkur, on our balcony.

"I've been waiting forever," he said with a sharpness that was cancelled out by his grin. "You two didn't stop to . . . Alright, I guess I don't want to take the conversation in that direction."

For a male who'd recently ended his relationship with his father, he was much too cheery. Although sorrow lingered in his eyes.

We went inside, and my brother explained that his advisors had captured a dresalod during the prior attack, and it was being held in a seawater tank for study.

"I believe we need to test which works, the boiling water or the herb, don't you?" he asked Rhoslyn.

I appreciated that he included her in the conversation as an equal. If anything, she was far above us, having discovered a solution to our problem.

"I can make a cup, and we'll bring both." She hurried to the kitchen, returning not long after with a covered cup of hot water and a packet of lindenmint. "I'm ready."

We walked to the laboratory built into the side of the seawall where Madr's advisors held the dresalod, and my heart stilled to see it floating in a tank, glaring at us.

"Can you drain some of the water?" Madr asked his advisor who was hovering nearby, wringing his hands.

"Of course, my prince."

"Just Madr." His sigh bled out, but I didn't sense any regret. "I've disowned my father. The throne. All of it."

"What?" The advisor reeled backward, his arms lifting. "This isn't possible."

"Yet I've done it."

"I would advise you not—"

"It's done," Madr growled.

The advisor bowed. "Very well, your . . . I cannot call you anything else except my prince." His hands fluttered at his throat in panic.

"Lower the water level please."

The advisor turned one of the dials on the side of the tank, and the water dropped quickly. "How much?"

"Until the dresalod is fully exposed," I said.

Rhoslyn watched raptly, the water and packet of herbs in her hands.

When the water had dropped enough, the advisor turned the dials again. The dresalod clawed at the inside of the tank, trying to rake its way through. From the hunger in its eyes, it would rip us apart and eat us within seconds.

"Here." Rhoslyn extended the water and herbs toward my brother.

He gave her a solemn look. "I'd like you to do the honors if you don't mind, sister."

"All right." She strode over to the tank and studied

the dresalod through the glass for a moment. "Such a dangerous beast. If only it could offer us peace." She stepped up onto a block beside the tank and took the lid off the water. A jerk of her arm, and the liquid splashed onto the dresalod.

It flinched, but nothing else happened.

"Hmm," she said, untying the top of the packet of herbs. "Let's hope this works, then." She poured a large pack of ground lindenmint over the side. It poured down onto the dresalod.

Shrieking, the creature writhed, its exoskeleton smoldering. It tumbled onto its side and twitched as the herb ate through its hard, protective outer shell, killing it almost as fast as I could with my mace.

"Well," she said, her voice shaky. "As a healer, I don't like to kill anyone, but in this case, I have to admit, I'm grateful this worked." She hopped off the box and stepped into my waiting arms, looking up at me. "I think it's time to start transplanting lindenmint plants to the shore, don't you?"

CHAPTER 41
RHOSLYN

Two Weeks Later

It took us over a week to dig up enough lindenmint bushes and plant them along a long stretch of shore from above the city to well below. We suspected we'd have to transplant more, covering considerable distance in both directions, but for now, this was a test. We were confident the herb would help us, but would it stop the dresalods? We'd find out during the next attack.

Since the herb was so prevalent, we dried huge bunches of leaves and scattered them along the shore above the waterline as well. And we set up small catapults that would launch lindenmint slurry carefully wrapped in thin membranes that would break on impact.

"For the first time, I have hope we can defeat them," Jaus said as we stood on the top of the wall with our friends who'd helped us complete the work. "You gave us this gift, tiny mate, and we'll never be able to thank you."

Around us, orcs grunted in agreement. I'd made friends, so many, and I'd found a home. I missed my sister, but we'd talked about visiting the fortress. Jaus and Feyla would take me there, and I'd ask Kael to notify my sister I was waiting outside the wall. It would be wonderful to see her again, to hug her once more. I couldn't wait to hear about her wedding plans and the future she planned with her love.

"If they come now, they'll quickly discover we fight back in unusual ways," Jaus growled.

With nothing left to do but wait, we left the wall.

"I'll see you at the party tonight?" Madr asked at the base of the stairs.

"We have other plans." Jaus squeezed my hand. After working hard each day over the past few weeks to get things ready along the shore, we'd dropped into bed exhausted each night. We'd talked about spending this evening alone.

"I'll see you another time, then." Madr told us he was going to permanently move to his mother's modest home high in the mountains. It was rustic, but he liked doing things for himself and the solitude he'd found there. He hadn't spoken to his father since he left the palace weeks ago, and I didn't think he ever would. If a bridge was going to be built between them, the king would have to lay the first stones.

Madr's gaze traveled from Jaus to me, noting our entwined fingers, and the longing in his gaze made my heart ache. He'd wistfully told me days ago that he'd hoped to find a mate during the next hunt. He'd represent his clan again in a year, but he'd have to wait until then and hope his Lumen Clan pendant flared for one of the two women.

To think I'd been frightened when I volunteered. Not only scared, but I'd also been horrified at the thought of being captured and claimed by an orc. Funny how things turn out as they should.

I suspected one of these times, the fates would choose a great love for Madr, and I couldn't wait to meet her. I hoped she was bold enough to give him a chance, to love him as he deserved.

Madr stopped at the base of the stairs leading to the top of the wall. "All right then. I hope you have a great evening."

I gave him a hug and watched as he strode toward the center of town. "I feel bad for your brother."

Jaus scoffed. "Why?"

"He's lonely."

"He has friends. You. Me."

"And you're certainly amazing."

He snorted.

"You are."

"You, my lovely one, are jaded."

I grinned up at him. "I have a good reason, don't I?"

Pausing, he kissed me. "You do."

I linked my arm through his, and we started walking toward our home. "Do you think he and the king will ever repair their relationship?"

He shrugged. "That's up to them."

Madr had made his peace with his decision. Only the king could change things between them. He'd have to work hard to earn the right to Madr's friendship.

"I hope the next hunt gives him a lovely woman who'll love him forever."

"You're sweet to say that." Stopping, Jaus turned me toward him. He stroked my cheeks with his thumbs then kissed me again. My belly fluttered and with a moan, I pressed myself against him.

He growled and lifted me up, deepening our kiss while pressing me against the wall of a building. I loved how I could make him lose control, how we couldn't keep our hands off each other.

We broke apart, grinning at each other.

"You need to get me home, mate," I said.

"Indeed I do." He lifted me into his arms and raced through the streets, taking the back stairs three at a time. Inside our tower home, he kicked the door shut, tossed his mace across the room, and took me to our bedroom. He laid me on the bed and crawled over me, holding my face while staring at me in a dreamy way.

"Love you so much, precious one," he growled.

"Love you too."

We pawed off our clothing and both sighed when skin met skin.

Watching my face, he ran his hands up and down my body, exploring every inch of me. His touch was electrifying, sending sparks of pleasure through my veins. I shivered as he stroked me, his fingers tracing circles on my belly and then moving lower to the apex of my thighs. He kissed me again, pressing me into the mattress as his tongue caressed mine.

Cupping my breast, he teased the nipple with gentle strokes until it hardened, and I whimpered with need beneath him. Leaving my mouth, he kissed down my neck, nibbling hard enough I suspected he'd leave a pink mark. Branding me as his alone. His soft lips moved across my collarbone, and a trail of goosebumps rose across my skin. His mouth continued its journey lower and lower until he reached his destination between my legs. As he sucked on my clit, wave after wave of pleasure crashed over me, a tidal force that could not be slowed.

I grabbed onto the sheets tightly as Jaus slowly brought me higher and higher, his mouth and teeth finding each pleasure point and giving it focus. He slipped his fingers inside me, and I jerked my hips up, crying out my joy.

He kept up the pace, drawing out my pleasure until I was close to the edge. I screamed out his name as an orgasm washed over me, feeling like I could stay there forever. Jaus didn't stop though; he kept going until he'd wrung everything out of me, and then he kissed his way back up my body.

He flipped me over onto my belly, lifting me onto my knees. His hard length pressed against my entrance. He slowly slid himself inside me, bit by delicious bit. I gasped as he filled me completely, the sensation almost too much to bear. He began to move, thrusting deep and slow. Leaning over me, his hands found mine, and he laced our fingers together.

Each of his thrusts sent heat and need blasting through me. Every nerve tingled with anticipation as Jaus sped up his rhythm, pushing us both closer and closer to the cusp of something wonderful. As I gave in, letting the sensations ripple through me, he went faster. His body tensed, and he let out a loud groan that echoed across the room like thunder.

We lay there for a moment afterwards, panting and shaking with pleasure until we finally came back down from our high. Jaus rolled off me and pulled me against his chest, wrapping his arms around me from behind.

"You stun me, tiny mate," he whispered into my hair before pressing a kiss on top of my head.

I smiled and snuggled into him, drifting to sleep.

I woke to Jaus shifting behind me and a hoarse cry outside. "They're coming!"

Shrieks echoed the guard's call, as did the blowing of a horn. Dresalods were attacking.

Jaus's arms tightened around me but only for an instant before he slipped from the bed and started dressing. "I must go."

"We'll both go." I wanted to see if our work over the past few weeks would make a difference. If the linden-mint plants and leaves on the shore had no effect, what could we try next?

My throat tightened at the thought that we might've worked for many days only to see no difference.

In no time, I'd tugged on a dress and stuffed my feet into my shoes.

Jaus stroked my face, his worried gaze sinking into mine. "You should stay here where it's safe, love. Please. If I'm battling with Feyla, I cannot be distracted. My fear for you would eat me alive."

"I could go to the wall." I shook my head and gave him a wry smile. "Our friends won't arrest me this time. They'll watch over me. I'll be safe there. If any dresalods climb the wall, I promise I'll run down the stairs and keep going until I'm safely inside our home."

He gnashed his tusks, but I could see he was relenting.

"I'll be safe. Truly." Since the creatures couldn't access our building, I could hide—something I hated to do while my friends and beloved mate battled to keep us safe.

No place was completely secure within the city, but

short of moving far away, where the shaydes might attack instead, there was no place we could go where something dangerous might not find us.

He grumbled with indecision. "I must leave. They're battling already, and they need me."

"Promise me you'll do all you can to come home to me, Jaus. I can't bear the thought of losing you."

He lifted me up, and we kissed with desperation. He was the world to me. How could I go on if something happened to him?

With a heavy heart, I followed him down the two flights of stairs to the first floor of our home. While he secured his mace to the sheath on his spine, I slid the blade Madr gave me into the sheath at my waist.

"I have protection." It wasn't much against a dresa-lod, but I'd put up a good fight.

With a growl that told me he wanted to argue but didn't have time, he took my hand and led me out onto the balcony. Feyla was already waiting, nervously gnashing her teeth and scraping her claws across the stone.

Dresalods shrieked on the seashore, and from the sound of it, many legions were attacking. Had they sent a huge force this time? I suspected they must've. As if they knew we were seeking a permanent solution, they'd come to defeat us once more.

With me in his arms, Jaus leaped onto Feyla. At his nudge, she took flight, soaring toward the wall where orcs bristling with weapons stood watching the advance of more dresalods than I'd seen in my life.

"So many," I whispered, the wind grabbing my words and sweeping them away. "How will we fight them all off if the lindenmint doesn't work?" A few of the orcs on the wall heard us coming and turned. One cheered, which was heartening, though maybe they were just glad to see Jaus.

He guided Feyla down until she could snatch one of them up with her claws if she wished. A jump, and he landed squarely on the stones. He lowered me to my feet and cupped my face, his stark with desperation. "Remain here where you have protection. If a dresalod makes it past the lindenmint, you run to our home. Am I making myself clear?"

I nodded. "Stay safe. Come back to me, mate."

"Always." He kissed me and stroked his knuckles down my cheek, staring at me as if he needed to memorize my face. Turning, he sprang onto Feyla's back and took flight, soaring toward the attacking dresalods with his mace lifted.

I raced to the edge of the wall and peered down. Numerous creatures surged through the waves, their claws lifting and clacking. My skin prickled with fear, and the memory of one stabbing my leg raked through me, making fear crawl up my spine.

One of the orcs stood beside me, watching as well. "See? They approach the herb. Will it work? We must pray to the fates."

I clutched the stone wall and held my breath.

The line of dresalods crossed the section where we'd scattered lindenmint on the sand.

They shrieked and started spinning, their limbs smoldering. One fell onto the herb, and it writhed, its large shell burning through. Others clambered up over their fallen brethren and scrambled toward the wall, their gazes locked on us watching. Fury darkened their eyes, and my lungs froze. They knew we'd done this, and they'd come for revenge.

Should I leave now?

Feyla and other voxes swooped down, the warriors on their back driving weapons through the dresalod legions, killing many. Jaus led them all, and I'd never been prouder of my mate. He was strong, determined, and clever.

He'd come back to me. Please.

The advancing dresalod army reached the shrubs we'd so carefully planted. We'd laid three rows, alternating the spacing, creating a wall as tall as my chin. With careful watering, they'd taken root, and if this worked, we'd make sure they not only multiplied but that they were cherished and well-tended.

When the dresalods started weaving among the shrubs, the thick leaves brushed against their hides. Instantly, their exoskeletons started smoking. They writhed, shrieking, and those coming behind them floundered, backing toward the sea.

Voxes waited, and those dresalods who weren't

dying from contact with the plant didn't make it to the water. Jaus and his team decimated them, leaving only dead creatures behind.

Soon, there were no more dresalods attacking.

A cheer rang up from the orcs on the wall around me, and it was echoed across the city.

Feyla flew close and Jaus leaped off her back, landing beside me.

He strode over to me, slipping his mace into the sheath on his spine.

"You're safe," I cried.

"I couldn't do anything else but return to you, tiny mate." Tipping my chin up, he gave me a quick kiss and a grin. "You've done it, love. You've gifted our people with a chance to live."

As he kissed me, I drank in the ongoing cheers of our friends.

When I took my sister's place in the Monster Mate Hunt, I never dreamed I'd find happiness or love.

Now, I'd found it with these people.

And with the love of my precious mate, Jaus.

Two Months Later

We rode on Feyla as she flew above the forest. We'd left the city yesterday evening, traveling all night, then spending the day in the meadow where we'd stayed after I claimed my lovely mate during the Hunt, then continued traveling in the early evening. We had a few hours left before the sun set and we'd need to start back.

As we approached the fortress, Rhoslyn's hands shook.

I leaned over and kissed her temple. "Why are you frightened, tiny mate?"

"I'm more nervous than scared." She sighed. "I've missed my sister so much. What if she's forgotten about me?"

"How could she? You're incredible. Amazing."

She sent me a smile over her shoulder. "I love that you still adore me."

I tightened my arms around her. "I feel the same."

Leaning into my chest, she sighed again. "Lyneth must be married by now."

"This is good, isn't it?"

"It is. She could even be pregnant like me."

I stroked her still flat belly, something I did whenever I could. While lying in our bed. Sitting in the tub (and while she rode my cock while I sat in the tub). And even when we sat at our table eating our meals. As she said, I adored her. And I couldn't want to hold our orcling who'd be a bit of both of us. We believed she'd gotten pregnant our first time together.

"When I lived behind the walls, I thought that was the entire world," she said.

"You said you went to the forest almost daily to collect herbs."

"None of us go there at night."

"Until the Hunt."

"Especially during the Hunt."

I chuckled. "You feared the mighty orcs."

"How could we not? We can't kill even a single shayde without losing three or four of our number, but orcs can take out three of them with one sweep of a mace."

"*I* can take out three of them with one sweep of my mace. Every other orc will need at least two blows."

Her laugh snorted out, and her spine loosened, which was my intention with my joke. "There's the orc I know and love." She leaned back in my embrace. "My sister was my world until I had to leave her. Do you think she'll be mad at me?"

"You bravely stepped into what you thought was a horrible situation in order to save her. How could she be angry about that? She loves you."

"As much as I do her. We were all the other had after our parents died. I protected her always. Then I had to leave her, and they wouldn't even let me say goodbye."

"I'm sure she understands."

"I hope so."

I guided Feyla down toward the ground to land in an open meadow not far from the fortress, where we slid off her back.

Rhoslyn stroked Feyla's long snout and gave her a kiss on the forehead. "No one has ever returned from the hunt."

"Which must make it seem even more terrifying."

"You wouldn't believe the horrible things my people say about orcs, the stories they tell about what might happen to the unfortunate women who run through the woods with orcs chasing them."

I wrapped my arms around her from behind. "They must think we harm them when all we wish to do is love them."

"At least I can tell them the truth about that."

I turned her in my embrace and kissed her gently. "Are you ready, my little one?"

Biting down on her lower lip, she nodded.

Holding hands, we traveled through the woods, taking a wide path that mostly let us walk side by side. When we reached the edge of the forest, we stopped, gazing across the big open field between here and the fortress.

Then we stepped out into the sunshine together.

As we drew closer, shouts rang out from the top of the wall, and a smile grew on my pretty mate's face.

"It's going to be all right," she said. "I'm so excited!"

We stopped before we reached the gate. When the guards pointed bows our way, I was tempted to pull my mace, but I resisted. They'd be foolish to fire upon us. That would risk the treaty we'd signed that gave them the protection they needed.

"It's Rhoslyn," a male cried out.

Rhoslyn startled. "Kael? Is that you, Kael?"

"Is that orc harming you, Rhoslyn?" Kael shouted. "Because I'll . . ." His voice softened. "Please tell me he hasn't hurt you."

She squeezed my hand. "This is my mate, Jaus. We met during the Hunt, and I couldn't be happier that he found me."

My low chuckle rang out. "You fought me from the moment we met, love," I said softly. "You were not happy then."

She shot me a grin. "I fought you because you were grumpy and growly."

"Not any longer."

"You're my cinnamon roll hero now."

"Forever," I vowed.

She turned back to the gate. "I've come to see my sister. Could you send Lyneth out?"

"It's not a trick, is it?" Kael asked, his grim gaze meeting mine. He was old, but I suspected he was a seasoned warrior. He'd be no match for an orc, but I respected that he wanted to protect my Rhoslyn.

"No trick. We're here for a peaceful visit. Please, can I speak with Lyneth?" Rhoslyn asked. "Send her out."

"We'll see if she wants to speak with you," someone yelled.

Shortly after that, a woman's voice rang out from behind the gate. "Let me see her. Rhoslyn. Rhoslyn! Please tell me she's safe."

Rhoslyn leaned into my side. "It's my sister. She's coming." She lifted her voice. "I'm safe. Come out to see me, Lyneth!"

The gate creaked open and two guards bristling with weapons stepped out, followed by a female a few years younger than Rhoslyn. She had my love's same golden hair and blue eyes, plus her smile that wavered when her gaze landed on me.

She clutched a knife as she stalked closer. Her hand lifted, and she whispered, "Run to me, Rhos. I'll hold him off with the knife, and we'll escape inside the fortress. He won't dare the village attack alone."

"This is my mate, my husband, Lyneth," Rhoslyn said with a laugh. "Please put your knife down. There's no place I'd rather be than by his side."

Lyneth froze, frowning. "You . . . care for this orc?"

"He's wonderful. Adoring. He treasures me above all others, and just as much, he loves me. I love him too." Her hand rested on her belly. "We're going to have an orcling. Can you believe that? You'll be an aunt."

Lyneth swallowed hard, and the knife fell from her limp hand, thudding on the grass by her feet. "You *love* him?" Her gaze searched mine, and whatever she saw there seemed to reassure her. Her shoulders curled forward, and she gasped out a breath.

"I'm Jaus," I said, giving her a bow.

"Err . . ." She swallowed hard. "I'm Lyneth."

"Tell the women who run through the woods that the mate hunt is a chance to meet an orc who will love them forever," Rhoslyn said.

"It can't be true." Lyneth's voice croaked. "Can it?"

"It is." Rhoslyn held out her arms. "Get over here, little sis. I need a hug."

"Rhoslyn," Lyneth cried. "I've missed you so much."

Lyneth rushed to my mate, and they held each other and cried. Thankfully, their tears soon dissolved into laughter.

When they parted, Lyneth stared up at me. "I'm still not sure what I think about orcs."

"We're quite amazing," I said. "I assure you."

Rhoslyn laughed. "And this one is quite conceited, I *assure you*. But I adore him so much."

Lyneth held her hand out to me. Rhoslyn had told me the clasping of palms was a human way of solidifying an introduction.

Taking her hand, I bowed low toward her again. "It's an honor to meet you. My mate speaks of you often. She's missed you."

"I . . ." A smile flitted across Lyneth's face, and she blushed. "I'm honored to meet you, too, Jaus." Her smile grew as her gaze met Rhoslyn's. "He's quite handsome, isn't he? I've only seen orcs from a distance. He's . . . big. Very muscular."

Rhoslyn leaned into my side. "He's kind and gentle too."

"Would you like to come inside the fortress?" Lyneth gestured toward the gate. "We can visit longer. Things . . . have happened."

"Is everything all right?"

Lyneth squeezed her eyes shut for a moment, and when she opened them, tears gushed out, streaming down her face. "I lost my husband to a fever a month ago. It's been terrible, Rhos. I wasn't sure how to go on after that."

"Oh, sister." Rhoslyn hugged Lyneth again, and they cried together once more. "We can't come inside. You know how the others will react to an orc in their midst."

"They don't know what we do." Lyneth's eyes met mine. "I'm sorry I didn't greet you as I should. You will always find welcome in my home, brother."

"Thank you. We're big, greenish, and fearsome. I can understand why you might hesitate to trust us for anything beyond providing protection."

"Not any longer." She rushed over to me and hugged me, and I grinned at my mate, who nodded with new tears in her eyes.

When we parted, I tugged Rhoslyn into my embrace.

Lyneth watched us with approval. "I'm glad you came to see me. I've missed you so much, Rhos, but knowing you're happy with Jaus makes me feel much better."

"She's my tiny mate, my precious wife," I said.

"I can see that now."

Lyneth and Rhoslyn embraced once more, and Lyneth slowly walked back to the fortress, picking up her knife as she passed it. She turned before entering the gate and blew Rhoslyn a kiss.

"We'll come back again after our orcling is born," Rhoslyn called out. "You need to meet him or her."

"I cannot wait!" Lyneth stepped inside, and the gate banged closed behind her.

"I'm so glad I got to see my sister," Rhoslyn said, turning in my embrace. She gave me a smile full of sadness and joy. "But I think it's time for us to go home, don't you, Jaus?"

I swept her up in my arms and carried her back into the woods.

Before we flew home, we'd stop at her parents' grave to leave flowers since it was outside the fortress walls.

CHAPTER 43

EPILOGUE
RHOSLYN

The Evening Before the Next Hunt

Our friends joined us on the balcony for a party. We gathered together a lot, celebrating the ongoing success of the linden-mint plants and the security we'd found within our city.

While we still used the balcony for Feyla's landing spot, we'd also furnished the broad space with a sofa, chairs, and tables, and we loved lounging together here at night, gazing at the stars.

Eleri sat with Odik, their one-month-old daughter, Yusta, sleeping in her lap. His arm was wrapped around her shoulders, and he seemed oblivious to anyone but them. Their young son played with toys nearby.

Madr lifted his drink in a toast. "To the Mate Hunt.

May this year's males prove as successful as prior years." His gaze met each of ours with considerable longing as he fingered the Lumen Clan pendant hanging around his neck. Shaped like the sun, it represented the mountains and heavens above. "May my clan's pendant glow for me." He directed his eyes to his drink.

I hoped he was chosen this year. He might bluster when I asked how he was doing, telling me he was fine, happy even, but I could tell he was lonely. He enjoyed living high in the mountains, visiting us often, but who wouldn't want a treasured mate by their side? Of course, I wanted all our friends to find love and happiness with a partner. We all deserved to have someone special in our lives.

Shirra stirred in my lap, and I smiled down at my precious orcling child. At two-months-old, she had Jaus's lovely berry-tinged hair and greenish-gold skin. Her features and body were more delicate like mine, and her eyes were my bright blue. Since they were so close in age, Eleri and I expected our daughters to grow up best friends.

She woke and started gurgling and kicking her feet. A happy baby, she barely made a fuss from morning until night.

"Finally, our little princess awakens," Madr exclaimed, putting down his drink and scooping Shirra up from my arms.

He kept insisting she was in line for the throne, but we just shook our heads. The king had not replied to the note we sent him announcing her birth, and he still did not acknowledge Jaus as he should.

"Would my gorgeous niece like to take a stroll with her uncle?" With her cuddled in his arms, Madr walked slowly around the outside of the balcony, pointing out landmarks to Shirra who drooled and stared up at him with adoration.

"Will you have more orclings?" Eleri asked me.

"We thought we'd wait until Shirra is walking," Jaus said.

As a healer, I was familiar with herbs that would prevent pregnancy, and I'd take them until we were ready to have another orcling. I'd also shared them with my friends. We all adored our mates and our children, but it was nice to have a choice of how many orclings we delivered.

"We also want to wait until we're fully moved into my estate in the foothills of the mountains," Jaus added.

"You're renovating this building, correct?" Odik asked, waving to the balcony in general.

I nodded and took a sip of my drink. "The shop-keeper on the lowest level moved his business, and we need the room for times we visit the city."

"Now that we no longer need to fear the dresalod attacks, we can live on the ground floor as well," Jaus said. "We'll move our kitchen and living quarters to the first level and add bedrooms in the area where the kitchen and living area are right now."

"You're going to love having two homes," Eleri said,

leaning into Odik's side. "It rarely gets hot when you live near the sea. The ocean breezes keep you cool. And you can spend other times of the year in the hills."

"How goes the lindenmint plantings?" Odik asked. "We've planted them along the cliffs all around the island. Once they're rooted well, the usual storm doesn't appear to disturb them. They're hearty, which is just what we need."

Now that Jaus didn't have to spend as much time battling dresalods, he'd shifted his and his soldiers' focus to transplanting the shrubs that had not only saved our lives but provided ongoing protection. The dresalods kept reproducing, but at least they could no longer reach us. Each time they left the sea, they encountered the herb and vast numbers of them realized their mistake.

"We've planted lindenmint shrubs for many cliks below the city and are slowly working our way north," Jaus said. "We've discovered something else interesting about the dresalods, however."

We all listened eagerly.

"Their numbers are going down."

"Really?" Odik exclaimed. He took their daughter from Eleri and laid her across his shoulder, patting her back while she continued to sleep.

"My idea's working, correct?" I said, smiling at Jaus. "I know you were skeptical."

"I always listen to you, mate."

I chuckled. "Not at first."

He leaned over and kissed my nose before shooting

everyone a grin. "She's right, but I've learned the error of my ways. Now that we burn the dresalods carcasses and use the ashes to fertilize our fields, those still in the sea have less to eat. Less to eat means fewer dresalod young. We don't expect to eliminate them all, and we're not sure we should since they eat refuse off the bottom of the sea, keeping it clean, but it would be nice not to worry about them coming to shore again in such large numbers."

"To such a future," Odik said, lifting his glass.

We all did the same, hoping the fates would watch over us and give us a chance to live in peace.

Jaus smiled down at me and, curling forward, gave me a kiss.

To think I'd fought him from the moment I met him. Now, I couldn't imagine loving anyone more than him and our daughter. We'd soon visit my sister again to show off Shirra, and Madr came to dinner at least once a week.

I had a new life. A new family.

Snug in Jaus's embrace, there was no place I'd rather be.

Would you like to read a bonus epilogue
from Rhoslyn's point of view?
She and Jaus are going to visit Feyla's
nest and they're bringing her a few
surprises. I'd tell you what they are, but
I don't want to spoil the *secret*.

<u>Sign up for my newsletter</u>
<u>& I'll send you the bonus scene right away!</u>

Be sure to pick up
<u>Orc's Fate</u>, Madr's story.
Madr's late for the hunt. Will another male
beat him there and claim the woman he's
destined to love for the rest of his life?

And if you haven't received your FREE
copy of Orc's Mate,
the prequel story in the Monster Mate Hunt world,
sign up for my newsletter, &
get it now!

A new life, a new job, a new orc husband . . .
Wait, isn't he supposed to be my boss?

Find out what happens next
in <u>Candy For My Orc Boss</u>!

An orc science teacher is determined to
give me a lesson in chemical reactions.

Check out <u>Orc-us Pocus!</u>

And don't forget,
I've got a FREE BOOK just for YOU!
Sign up for my newsletter,
and I'll send you a copy of
<u>Escorting the Alien</u>

About the Author

Ava Ross is a two-time *USA Today* Bestselling author who has written numerous titles, all of them featuring sweet and steamy romance. She fell for men with unusual features when she first watched Star Wars, where alien creatures have gone mainstream. She lives in New England with her husband (who is sadly not an alien, though he is still cute in his own way), her kids, and a few assorted pets.

SERIES BY AVA

Mail-Order Brides of Crakair

Brides of Driegon

Fated Mates of the Ferlaern Warriors

Fated Mates of the Xilan Warriors

Holiday with a Cu'zod Warrior

Galaxy Games

Alien Warrior Abandoned/

Shattered Galaxies

Beastly Alien Boss

Bride of the Fae

A Sci-Fi Holiday Tail

Monsterville, USA

Monster on Board

(co-written with Alana Khan)

A Monster Worth Fighting For

(Monster Between the Sheets)

Love at First Orc

Monster Mate Hunt

Single Titles
Dad Bod Dragon
Mated to the Dragon
Jasmine's Enchanted Genie
Swamp Thing (You Make My Heart Sing)

You can find my books on Amazon.

ORC'S FATE

Can a lonely widow and an orc with secrets find true love together?

Lyneth

After my husband's death, my village pushes me into the forest during the monster mate hunt, where I'll be claimed as an orc's bride.

I've vowed I'll never love another, but then I'm claimed by Madr, a strong, handsome orc who I suspect is hiding secrets. On his dragon-like vox, he flies with me toward his home. His warm arms keep me safe, and his teasing touch makes me reconsider every assumption I made about my past and my future. Do I dare give my heart to an orc?

Madr

When I abdicated the orc throne, I planned to live a simple life. I never expected the fates to bind me to Lyneth or that I'd fall for her so fast. But someone's out to kill me, and if I don't stop them, I won't survive long enough to claim my new bride.

Orc's Fate is Book 2 in the Monster Mate Hunt Series. Expect a seductive orc prince with a creative. . . (cough), size difference, her awakening, only one bed/forced proximity, a mourning woman finding new love, fated mates, plus a fantasy world you'll want to live in. HEA guaranteed. Each book is standalone but the series is more fun if read in order.

Books in Order:

Orc's Mate

(a prequel novel – FREE with newsletter sign-up)

Orc's Craving

Orc's Fate

Orc's Maiden

Orc's Captive

Orc's Taming

CHAPTER 1
LYNETH

Tonight, I would have to give my body and soul to a fearsome orc.

Each year for the past eleven, my village sent two women into the forest to be claimed by orcs in exchange for protection from horrifying creatures called the shaydes.

The shaydes would kill us. As for the orcs?

They wanted to *mate* with us.

"It's time," Guardsman Kael said sadly. He laid a hand on my shoulder, squeezing gently. "Say the word and I'll do all I can to keep this atrocity from happening. There are other villages far from here. Would run. Hide. It would keep you safe."

I hadn't volunteered for the hunt like my sister had one year ago. No, they'd shoved me, a widow, to the top of the list, and when the two names were announced in the village square, mine was spoken first.

"I don't mind," I said, packing the rest of my few belongings. My deceased husband, dear man though he was, had not possessed much, and I'd come to our marriage with even less. "Actually, I almost welcome leaving the memories of Sveth behind. I see him every-where. I hear his voice right behind me, calling to me. Yet when I turn, he's not there." It shattered me each time.

"Better to face a ghost of someone you loved than lie beneath a rutting orc," Kael snarled.

One male rutting was pretty much the same as the next, wasn't it? Not that I had much experience, just that of my husband. After the initial pain, the rutting wasn't terrible. Sveth hadn't pushed me for relations more than once a week. Perhaps if he had, I might've been with child when he got sick and died. At least then, I'd have a memory of him to hold close.

Instead, my arms remained empty.

"There's nothing for me here any longer except for you, dear friend," I said. If Kael hadn't taken me in after Sveth died, I wasn't sure what might've happened to me. Sveth's home was claimed by his family who hadn't held me in high regard. Women cannot own property, they'd claimed. Kael spoke up for me, but our evil mayor, Eamon, had insisted I must leave the home I'd only lived in for two months. "I'll miss you horribly, but this is for the best. Someone needs to go. Why not me?"

"No woman should have to contemplate a future with an orc."

"I'm not afraid," I said, though even I could hear the

tremor in my voice. "Remember, my sister said the orcs are kind."

Kael drew himself up, crossing his arms on his chest. "I'm not convinced."

"The decision has been made." I flung the strap of my bag over my shoulder, and none too soon.

Eamon banged on the door. "Time to leave. The sun has set. The orcs wait."

"He takes too much pleasure in this," Kael said softly.

I dropped my bag and hugged him. This was likely the last time I'd see him. Rhoslyn's orc mate had brought her to visit me months ago, but I doubted anyone would bring me here to visit Kael.

"Take care, friend," I said. "Thank you for all you've done for me."

"*You* take care," he said. "You're the one who needs it most."

He followed me from his small home. As I passed through the solemn crowd who'd gathered to witness our sacrifice, a few touched my arm, wishing me well. Most watched with relief in their eyes. For this year, *they* were safe.

Alwen stood with her mother beside the gate. When she heard me approaching, she turned her steely gaze my way. Some villagers scorned her, because she wore pants like a male, and she hunted, something no other women did. If anyone could escape the orcs and find a way to survive in the forest, it would be her.

I nodded as I passed her and took the bag waiting for

me beside the gate. They were packed for those chosen, and while the clothing would be too loose on my lean frame, I wouldn't turn down the chance for a few more outfits. Only the fates knew when I'd be offered more.

"Shall we walk together?" I asked Alwen, who nodded grimly. She shot a dark look at her father. "Perhaps we can protect each other." Though I doubted even she'd be much good against a fearsome orc. At nearly twice our size, any of them could knock us to the ground with one blow if they wanted.

Only when I contemplated what was about to happen did my heart freeze. Could I remain strong and hold back my shrieks when an orc claimed me?

It appeared I was about to find out.

With a nod to Kael and Alwen's mother, I walked with Alwen to the gate and through the tiny opening the guards created to allow us to pass.

We hurried across the big open stretch of grass between the village's high fortress walls and the forest. My heart thudded too quickly in my ears, and my breathing came out overly loud, ragged.

"Stay close with me, and you might just survive this," Alwen whispered. Her hand went to the knife sheathed at her side. "I have a weapon, and I'm not afraid to use it." She pulled it. Brandished it with a feral look in her eyes.

An chitter echoed from the forest. Damn, there were shaydes nearby. They hunted at night, and we would soon be their prey. Would it be better to be killed by one of them or lie beneath a rutting orc?

I swallowed deeply, but I couldn't get anything past the lump of terror in my throat.

We entered the woods, leaving the relative safety of the moonlit field behind.

Guttural cries rang out somewhere in the distance.

Alwen shot me a dark look and nodded. "Remember. Stay with me. Don't fall behind." She bolted into the woods, and I started after her, but she was much too fast and I soon lost her in the dark.

I slowed my pace. Better to take care where I placed my feet than stomp around and draw attention.

An orc would claim me whether I ran, walked, or laid on the ground and waited for him to arrive.

I didn't care one bit how it came about.

It wasn't like I had anything left to live for.

Get Orc's Fate now!